RUBY RED

Natalie Buske Thomas

ISBN-13: 978-0615959764

ISBN-10: 0615959768

This book is a work of fiction.

All events and dialog are for entertainment purposes only and do not necessarily represent the author's views

To Brent, Cassandra, Nicholas and
Savannah

RESEARCH CREDITS

Einstein 1905: The Standard of Greatness by John
S. Rigden, Harvard University Press,
ISBN 0-674-01544-4

Albert Einstein by Kathleen Krull,
ISBN 978-0-670-06332-1

*Something Incredibly Wonderful Happens: Frank
Oppenheimer and the World He Made Up*, by K.C. Cole,
ISBN 978-0-15-100822-3

The Science of Sherlock Holmes by E.J. Wagner,
ISBN 978-0-471-64879-6

*The Particle at the End of the Universe: How the
Hunt for the Higgs Boson Leads Us to the Edge of a New
World* by Sean Carroll, Dutton,
ISBN 978-0-525-9535-9-3

*Hidden Evidence: Forty True Crimes and How
Forensic Science Helped Solve Them* by David Owen,
Firefly Books,
ISBN 1-55209-483-9

The Grand Design by Stephen Hawking and
Leonard Mlodinow,
ISBN 978-0-553-80537-6

The Hidden Reality by Brian Greene, Alfred A.
Knopf, ISBN 978-0-307-26563-0

Why Does E=mc2? by Brian Cox and Jeff
Forshaw, DaCapo Press, ISBN 978-0-306-81758-8

AUTHOR'S WORKS

The Serena Wilcox Mysteries

The Serena Wilcox Time Travel Trilogy

Project Scarecrow, Ruby Red, Future Beyond

The Serena Wilcox Dystopian Trilogy

Angels Mark, Covert Coffee, Bluebird Flown

The Serena Wilcox Mysteries: Books 1, 2 & 3

Odd and raw novellas from 1998-2000

Gene Play, Virtual Memories, Camp Conviction

Other Books

Thriving in a Hateful World, Ramen Noodles and Hot Dogs,
The Miracle Dulcimer, The Magic Camera

Other Works

Oil paintings (most notably *Savannah Reading in the Butterfly Garden*), Natalie is also a singer/songwriter, public speaker and entertainer.

www.NatalieBuskeThomas.com

1

"I'm Serena Wilcox, former private detective, wife, and mother of three."

"Why is she introducing herself again? Do we have to go through this every time we get new staff?" Agent Estep also repeated himself every time they got new staff. This particular repartee had grown tiresome for the crew members who had by now heard the same dialogue nearly verbatim, ad nauseam.

"Agent Estep's objection aside, I'd love to get to know all new members of the Project Scarecrow crew." Serena crooked her finger and indicated that the new members should come to the front of the board room. When the three newcomers were standing beside her she continued.

"Our new additions come with serious credentials. The Gödel Solution Institute has of course captured the world's attention. Our first time travel mission revealed startling discoveries about people from the future. They are traveling through time alongside us, but separately from us, and they are not pleasant."

Beav said, "Serena, read the warning from your future self. Everyone needs to hear it word for word."

Serena nodded. "I memorized it. My future self said, 'They are evil. Do whatever it takes to stop them. Fear nothing. It's never too late to change the fate of the world.'

"I know that this doesn't tell us much. I'm assuming that I couldn't warn us in detail due to a paradox or something else that I don't understand. What we do know is that the time travelers of the future are malevolent. I'm not saying that we've been apathetic before now, of course not. We've been working like dogs for weeks. But it's time to fly into 'crisis mode'.

"We've officially dubbed our mysterious futuristic villains the MOTF, the 'Men of the Future', for lack of anything more creative. I do wonder though, won't we run across female travelers at some point, or has everyone assumed that we'll only see men from the future? I'd hate to think that women have

3

been set back to the point where none of the travelers of the future are women."

Beav made a basketball referee's sign for "traveling" to signal to Serena that she was rambling. If he didn't reign her in she was likely to jump from one tangent to the next, thinking aloud until someone finally snapped. He jerked his head toward the newcomers standing in the front of the room.

The first in line was shuffling his feet, the second was drumming his fingers on the podium, and the third added the final notes to the arrangement by cracking his neck in a cringe-worthy round of popping sounds. Serena invited the finger-tapper to introduce himself. The human band came to an abrupt halt as everyone shifted their attention away from Serena.

"I'm Archie Hollar. I'm replacing Malirah who is out of the country for her lavish tabloid wedding. She has decided not to return to GSI so I'm here permanently." There were a few murmurs from the crew. It was the first they'd heard of Malirah's decision and some were put off by this man's lack of social skills. "I'll be working behind-the-scenes as she did. I won't be doing any time travel missions. I see no point in standing up here." He sat down.

Serena added, "As Archie said, he'll be replacing Malirah on the GSI home team. We'll also be filling two other vacancies today, but that won't make up for everyone we've lost." She paused here, out of respect for the crew members who had died during the early days of Project Scarecrow.

After the silence grew uneasy she continued. "We'll be operating with a smaller crew for the foreseeable future." The two newcomers who were still standing at the front of the room looked at

Serena expectantly. She addressed their unspoken question. "Before I get to the other new members…" The newcomers' shoulders slumped.

"I should talk about who is staying on with us. Agent Estep is heading up the operation on the government-cooperative level, which includes the tactical aspects of our missions. Meanwhile Beav is managing from the GSI level, which includes the home base operations and the technology based…"

"I'm the techie gypsy. I manage the geeks." Beav bowed when his quip was rewarded with laughter.

Serena said, "On that note, I suppose that I should add that both Estep and Beav manage *me*." She too generated laughter, from all but Agent Estep, who didn't appreciate the joke in the slightest.

Serena continued. "Jo is staying on with us. She'll time travel with me on some of the missions. I'm not quite sure what else she'll be doing." She let this sentence dangle for a second. When it was clear that no one would jump in to explain what Jo was doing on the project, Serena moved on.

"Lehman has agreed to return to the Midwest next week. I think he's available for as long as we need him, as we have yet to find anyone who can be trusted with his level of security, at least no one else who has the skills that Lehman does. Anyway, Lehman understands the situation and he's made himself available to us, although I think he intends to fly back and forth on a regular basis, between GSI and his home in Texas. My point is, he might be hard to reach at times. Plan accordingly."

Serena paused when she heard one of the newbies clear his throat. She held up her index finger to indicate that she needed just one more minute.

She said, "As for historical research, you should continue to contact Professor Dr. Kendra Wellington with questions, or contact Nicholas at the lab if you want any research done for you. As for those who are leaving, I'm sad to say that James Edison Spector will not be continuing with us. They told me this morning that he has received another job offer. Eduardo Martin has also left us, as he has been recruited too, which has sucked the air out of me, I must confess. I'm not sure where he has gone, but there are whispers that he is working at a level of government that we aren't supposed to know exists. So, anyway, that leaves us with two more vacancies, in addition to the other losses we had during Project Scarecrow so far."

The neck-cracking newbie scoffed. "So far? No one dies on my watch."

Serena seized the opportunity to get back on task. "This is Buick. Most of us have already worked with him. He was on the production team that created Ruby Red. He's now part of the core crew. Welcome aboard, Buick!" Serena clapped. Her action inspired only tepid applause— not because people didn't like Buick, but because they had lost patience with Serena's long-windedness.

Serena smoothed her long dark hair behind her ears. She had forgotten to put her hair up in a ponytail before leaving the house. The hair distraction caused her to lose track of her thoughts.

When she remembered what she had been about to say, she resumed. "Both Beav and Estep will report to Buick, and he will report directly to Ann Kinji. Eduardo was sort of in this role, but it was never made official. Now the chain of command will be clear, which is something we should have done from the beginning. This should avoid some of the, how shall I put it? Posturing? Let's just say that Agent Estep and Beav need to stay in their own corners."

"Oh for pity's sake!" The third newbie blurted. "I have an appointment in fifteen minutes. This was supposed to be a short meet and greet. I'm Tara Clara. Yes, I know, it's a stupid name and it rhymes. I'm replacing James Edison. You won't see much of me because I'm on production crew and whatever else Beav needs me for. Rest assured, I'm here for Beav and no one else. I've been a big fan of his for years. I have no interest in any of this other business."

Beav gave Tara his signature two-fingered salute as she left. Everyone focused on the back of Tara's navy blazer until she disappeared from view. Serena said, "I'd say that this meeting went about as well as all of our others. I won't take this personally."

The crew popped out of their seats, but she stopped them. "Before the rest of you go, I do have one more issue to bring up. Eduardo's departure leaves a big gap. Buick is filling the managerial part of Eduardo's role here, but Eduardo was first and foremost our lead scientist. Buick can't fill those shoes, and we'll be hard pressed to find anyone who can. I'm not sure what Ann Kinji plans to do about it. I think she may be considering recruiting outside of the country."

Beav asked, "Why is this disconcerting? Don't we have all the data we need to continue without him?"

"No, we don't, actually. We are limited by how far back in time we can go. Remember, the MOTF wanted to go back further in time than our archived data allows. Because 1939 was one of the earliest time windows in our databank, they went back there with the express purpose of collecting more data to go to an earlier point in history that we didn't already have. And that's how they managed to turn up in World War 1 France—it was after they got the early data they wanted, remember?

"They used Eduardo to get that earlier data. If we need to travel further into the past, we also need him. So far, no one else knows how to retrieve data that's not already archived. It's a poor time for us to lose Eduardo as a resource. What if we need earlier data? Will we resort to doing what the MOTF had done, and go back in time to find Eduardo? That seems ridiculous when Eduardo should be on our crew, available to us in present time. He should be conducting this meeting instead of me."

"Now that I agree with," said Estep. He snorted and repositioned himself until his lanky body was sprawled across multiple chairs.

Serena waited for the clanging of the metal chairs to subside before continuing. "Also, there are gaps in our knowledge about time travel. There are troubling issues that were raised early on but those issues were never fully addressed. So what happens when we encounter these problem situations?"

"Like what? Be specific," said Buick.

Serena frowned. "Eduardo had explained that our data is comprised of what individuals heard, read, viewed, and sensed. Why would he have pointed that out? This is something that has nagged at me ever since he said it. I'm kicking myself that I didn't follow up on it and now it's too late to get answers."

Buick said, "I don't follow. Was I even there then? I attended only a few of the early meetings."

Serena reached for her purse. "He used an analogy. I wrote it down. Just a minute, let me read it to you." She rummaged past a half-empty bottle of ibuprofen, a collection of obsolete electronic keys, and a stash of old tissues before she finally dug an index card from the lint-infested bottom fold of her purse.

She strained to see the words on the card. She was unwilling to admit to herself that her near vision was failing. "I'm quoting word for word what Eduardo said, 'the memory of having read a letter would give us a reliable databank of what someone actually communicated, whereas the memory of a verbal conversation could be faulty due to the listener not hearing the spoken word correctly, or misinterpreting the meaning of what was said.'

"This scares me. Just because we've not yet encountered an incident of time travel distorted by faulty data, it doesn't mean that there won't be a first time. We have no safeguard against it, and no Eduardo to help us figure out what to do.

"And here's another thing: How will we even know if the experience is affected? Will we recognize the problem? What will happen to us if we time travel with faulty data? Will we end up in a fantasy alternate reality world? Will we die when we materialize into something that doesn't exist?"

Estep groaned. "You're already in a faulty fantasy world and you're not dead. If all you have left is theorizing, let me go."

Serena spoke faster. "No one seems at all concerned that we are utterly clueless about this potential pitfall. I see disaster. Why am I the only one bothered by this?" She searched the crew members' faces for any clue about what they were thinking. Their expressions were blank.

Beav said, "You left out the part about Hitler. That should get their attention."

"You take over, I'm losing my voice." Indeed, Serena's voice was barely above a whisper.

Estep said, "I knew it was going to be a good day when I got up this morning."

Beav ignored Estep. "When Serena and Jo were on the mission in World War 1, France, they interviewed soldiers who thought that the weapons of the future were something that Hitler created, but Hitler was only a corporal then. We've since analyzed the situation and we came up with a few ideas for this discrepancy.

"We're thinking that history may have been compromised by the MOTF, that's one theory. I hypothesize that the MOTF have already caused irreparable harm in ways that we can't begin to guess. Even the best coders can't guarantee that code won't go wonky. All it takes is new code mixed with old for a file to be corrupted. There's a file conflict or some explainable error, you know how it is. Errors result when we mess with original programming, making additions and deletions.

"But I'll offer up another theory. The WWI mission was understandably a high-stress environment. The crew was emotionally shaken during the debriefing and could have given us unreliable accounts. Mistakes may have been made. If the melding of history can be explained away by a simple misunderstanding, we have nothing to worry about.

"Another benign theory we raised is that even as a corporal, Hitler might have had something of a reputation, perhaps young recruits already feared him at that early stage. That's an unlikely explanation in my view. There's no historical evidence to support that theory.

"There's only one explanation that makes sense to me. The possibility that World War I and World War II have become historically blurred is overwhelming to think about, but we have to do it. I think we're talking about garbled code. When code goes rogue, anything can happen."

After captivating his audience, Beav abruptly shut down his train of thought. "I ran on here long enough, especially since we have no remedy for this anyway. Serena's right. We are in the pioneering stage of time travel technology. We aren't ready for these complications."

Silence fell. Serena resumed speaking, pushing past the strained grating quality in her voice. Several crew members cleared their own throats when they heard her speak. "Not to heap guilt on our heads, but we have to accept our own role in this as well. After all, we were there too. It's conceivable that it was the combination of the two sets of time travelers together in one space that caused a problem—if there is a problem. Beav's theory about altering the code after the original programming was set, and screwing it up that way, makes sense to me. But my pet theory is that too many travelers coming in from different directions, occupying the same time and space window, is the bigger issue. I imagine it to be like messing with the code, just by being where we don't belong, like it corrupts the existing code in some way. Does that make sense to you?"

No one responded. "Doesn't it make sense to avoid turning up in the same time window as the MOTF?" she asked.

Again, no one responded. Serena continued speaking, her voice now a mere squeak. "Well, I'll move on from that. We also have a limited time window situation, like I mentioned before, and that's already been a problem. Beav, please? I can barely talk."

Beav nodded. "As a refresher, or for the first time if you are new, I'll go off of Serena's playbook and quote Eduardo, 'Assuming that the newborn in question leads a normal healthy life and dies from natural causes, a single subject will offer us a memory window of about one hundred years into the future. These days it's not uncommon to discover lifespans of one hundred and fifteen years or more.'

"He was referring to brain tapping and collecting data from newborns and the elderly, to try to get the biggest time travel window possible. However, when the MOTF went back to 1939 and enlarged the time travel window, our eyes were opened to what future humanity is doing. They've made the time window into the future as far out as they've wanted to go, of course they have, what would stop them from doing it?

"The only reason why they needed us at all is because they couldn't go further back into the *past*. They were limited by our narrow archives and apparently our outdated technology restricted them from access. It makes me smile to think about how frustrated they must have been when they couldn't do what they wanted.

"But they don't need our data to push further into the future! How far have they gone? I don't think we have spent enough time thinking about what this might mean. They are more advanced than we are. We have no idea what they've been up to, dozens or hundreds of years into the future, maybe even thousands of years. Like Serena said, it's chilling how little we know. She posed these questions, 'Who are they? How far into the future are they? How much farther into the future have they traveled? Did they reach the end? Where have they been? What have they

21

done? What are they doing now? How do we find them? Are they watching us right now? Will we recognize them if we see them?"

"I agree with her that we are in over our heads in a mammoth way. I mean that both as in 'enormous' and literally 'prehistoric'."

Someone had given Serena hot tea with honey in it and she had been sipping it while Beav was speaking. Her voice was temporarily revived enough to finish out the meeting. She said, "How can we investigate what the MOTF are up to if we don't have Eduardo to guide us through the physics of all of this? I can't fully grasp today's science, let alone tomorrow's science and the science from light years into the future!

"I don't even know where to begin and I'm afraid that Project Scarecrow is at a level of urgency that we can't even wrap our minds around. We're in trouble, guys."

Serena finally had the crew's attention. She scrambled to finish up before she lost them again. "Eduardo had mentioned Einstein's field equations when he was explaining general relativity, in his explanation of how time travel technology originated. He said that Einstein's theory of relativity was published in 1915.

"Do you think it would benefit us if I went back to 1915 and talked to Einstein? If I were to pick his brain, and ask him theoretical questions, isn't it possible that he could enlighten us in some way? Namely, what I want to know is, can we fight against these MOTF or will we cause more harm than good? I'm thinking that Einstein will know if we can change history or not. I mean, he's the best we have, right? The fact that he's long dead isn't much of an obstacle. He's easier to find than Eduardo."

Everyone laughed. Serena didn't blink. The room filled with awkward quiet. Buick sauntered to the podium, relieving the tension. His stocky frame, his heft, and the shock of gray hair that outlined his temples were reassuring reminders of his maturity. He made eye contact one-by-one until he held them captive. Unlike Serena Wilcox, Buick's voice was strong, authoritative and unwavering.

He said, "The question you're all thinking is, why let Eduardo go if he's so critical? I'm warning you not to question Ann's leadership. If you don't trust her, you should leave now. If you don't trust me, you should leave now. If you don't trust your CC or your Director, you should leave now."

No one stirred.

Buick continued, "Project Scarecrow is unchartered territory. Doubts are dangerous. I trust all of you point-blank, and I'm asking you to do the same.

"Ms. Wilcox, people say that your ideas are crazy and will never work. Let me tell you about crazy. I've witnessed that 'crazy' works, particularly when there's nothing left to lose, and when no one else has any other ideas. And I believe that's the position we're in."

He glared at the crew members who had laughed the loudest at Serena. "It's that person willing to lay everything on the table who makes a difference. You have moxie and crazy in near equal proportion." Everyone's jaws dropped when Buick closed the meeting with the words, "Let's do it. Why not go to the best man for the job? Gear up, people. Ms. Wilcox, I'm signing off on your proposal. Ask Einstein."

Natalie Buske Thomas

2

The Gödel Solution Institute was bustling with activity. The chemistry of the newly organized crew was starting to gel, even though most of them would never become friends. New members Tara Clara and Archie Hollar were socially abrasive, but because no one had any reason to interact with them, nobody cared if they were friendly or not. Tara and Archie were on the production and technology team and they were seldom seen or heard. Their work made a difference, however, and they were valuable assets to the crew. Best of all, neither Tara or Archie had any history with Project Scarecrow, or with the government. For the first time since GSI had launched the crew felt safe around every member of the team. Safety was imperative, friendship was optional.

The GSI shake-up had also satisfied investors. Ann Kinji was more than happy to replace government-connected members with outsiders, which was familiar territory for her anyway. This is exactly what she had done when she was President of the United States. Ann insisted that what had worked to fix an impossible situation in Congress would certainly work for the relatively small staff of GSI. Ann's supporters agreed, and her approval rating was not at all dented by Project Scarecrow's disasters.

Nonetheless, Ann knew that the loyalty of the masses was fickle. They would easily turn on her if GSI had any more trouble with internal corruption. There could be no more hiccups! From now on, GSI employees would be under such close scrutiny that they couldn't so much as scratch their noses without cameras watching them. Ann oversaw the added security installation herself. Truth be told, the crew feared Ann much more than they feared the cameras. Had she known, she could have saved GSI thousands of dollars by tapping a wooden ruler in her hand while walking the halls.

The GSI crew adapted smoothly to the increased security measures. No one wanted a repeat of what had happened with Jorgi. They considered the ramped up surveillance to be less about restricting their personal freedom and more about keeping them safe. The fear of the MOTF was a common bond that stimulated unprecedented cooperation from the crew and a voluntary loss of freedom.

Weary of politics and internal strife, the crew was also invigorated by the idea of being one more step removed from the outside world. They had enough on their plates—who had time to worry about policy and the madness of the general public? That was Ann's arena, and now they had Buick as an additional buffer between the crew and GSI investors, media hounds, and the numerous government agencies breathing down their necks.

Buick was a buffer for internal squabbles too. During his first day in his new role, he smoothed ruffled feathers between active federal agent Estep and burned former agent Beav. The two men had served in the same operations time and time again, their missions spanning over a decade. They had racked up a comparable list of achievements and were evenly matched. But while Agent Estep had remained in the government's good graces and had received public recognition for his work, Beav had been scapegoated and demoted to the rank of private citizen. To say that tension had been thick between them was an understatement. Buick diffused that tension instantly by making one simple change. He gave both men a promotion in title, salary and even in company perks, such as each having their own VIP parking space in the GSI lot. Because their titles were distinctive, each man was given his own territory instead of butting heads over the same slice of pie.

Buick was confident that his promotion was a winning idea, but he was a realist. For extra measure, Buick had instructed the workers tasked with remarking the parking lot to place Estep's personal space on the opposite side of the building from Beav's – ditto for their new offices. Buick's diplomacy was an immediate success and the crew was relieved of the ongoing tension between the two men. That alone was enough to rejuvenate them.

Buick didn't stop there. Even Agent Estep's resentment about serving as a glorified bodyguard for Serena Wilcox had subsided. Project Scarecrow required government agency cooperation and Buick reminded Agent Estep that he was Ann Kinji's strongest link in the chain between the private sector and the government (or what Beav referred to as 'the regime'). Buick impressed upon Estep how important he was at GSI. He explained all of this as he promoted him to Commander in Chief, or Agent Estep, CC. Why, his protection of the world's first time travel investigator was nothing short of heroic!

Never mind that the title Commander in Chief was already taken, and was reserved for the President of the United States. No one cared one iota if Estep was CC or King of the World as long as he kept his snarly attitude out of the workplace.

Buick mimicked this same strategy when he promoted Beav. Beav's coworkers complained that he wasn't a team player. Indeed, he had a tendency to squirrel resources away and work on projects solo, pulling all-nighters to complete tasks without informing his team. While his work dazzled, he often missed the fine-tuning details that would have been attended to had he employed his esteemed colleagues instead of deliberately holding back on key information so he could finish projects alone. When Buick promoted Beav to Director he coached him on how to effectively lead his crew. Why, Beav was a natural manager! Buick's subtle manipulation technique worked wonders, as Beav was quick to embrace the idea of telling his crew what to do, thus his crew was now informed and involved in projects that Beav had previously cut them out of. Beav now saw his team as tools in his toolbox instead of as a threat.

Both Beav and Estep walked the halls of GSI with a new spring in their step. From day one of their new jobs, neither of these opinionated men had an impatient word, snarky quip, or random retort for anyone. Although the crew knew that this melody wouldn't play forever, they were grateful to Buick for every day of peace.

Buick, a father of eleven; nine biological children, two adopted, and dozens more he shepherded as a temporary crisis care provider, was a master coach for taming unruly children, confused young adults and, he chuckled, apparently spies and agents as well.

Naturally it helped that Buick was physically intimidating. His teddy-bear persona could turn on a dime and they knew it.

And so it was that the crew was off to a harmonious second beginning. But then again, none of them had seen Serena Wilcox yet that day. GSI had been clicking along amicably all morning without her.

Serena had arranged a flexible work schedule to spend more time at home with her family. The crew had almost forgotten that she was missing, as her presence was insignificant to their project goals. Nevertheless, within thirty seconds of her return, Serena unraveled all of the work that Buick had accomplished. All it took was this greeting, "I'm ready to meet with Einstein!"

Agent Estep, CC, and Director Beav talked over each other. Both objected to the mission to talk with Einstein. Words flew fast and furious as others chimed in. Their arguments ranged from the intellectual to the silly. Eventually insults were added to the mix and Buick came out of his office to see what was going on. He bellowed, "Enough! I approved this mission. She's going. She's going *now*!"

The crew dispersed. Beav scrambled to organize the production team. Under his direction, micro-management, and ultimately stepping in to finish the job himself, Beav's team created an authentic package for Serena's mission to meet Albert Einstein in 1915.

Beav assigned teen Nicholas the task of compiling a digital keyword-searchable packet on Einstein 1915, and anything else that they thought Serena might need to know. The entire packet was downloaded to Ruby Red's control panel and also to Serena's handheld gadget. She was well equipped for 1915 by late afternoon. The stony silence at GSI put hurry into everyone's steps.

Agent Estep put the Extreme A Team on standby. While no one anticipated that they would be called in, their readiness was now a requirement for every mission, even for operations that had been assessed as low risk like this 1915 mission. Until they knew more about what they were dealing with, Estep commanded his team to be indefinitely on alert from the conception of a mission to its debriefing.

The MOTF could be lurking behind every tree in the past, present and future— the Extreme A team was to be prepared to deploy within thirty seconds. The young soldiers of the Extreme team had renamed themselves the "Extremers" or "Xtremers", but GSI was slow to adapt. As they had only one military unit assigned to them, everyone knew who they were regardless of what people called them.

Production team and military command overshadowed the actual logistics of who was traveling. Those details seemed almost irrelevant to GSI. It was late in the day when they learned that Jo was unavailable to accompany Serena. Jo wasn't an ideal choice anyway. Her fair skinned, red haired, green eyed beauty was too attention-grabbing for the scholarly scene. They needed someone who could pass for a brilliant college student, and it just so happened that they had such a person on their freelance payroll. Since Nicholas was a fan of Einstein, and because he fit the profile for a young scholar, it was decided that he would accompany Serena.

The 1915 package was easy for the production team to assemble. Their cover story was obvious. Nicholas was a child prodigy who had entered college early, Serena was his mother. Neither of those two things was much of a stretch. With the cover story already checked off of their list, it looked like they would accomplish the mission before the end of the day, tomorrow at the latest. Buick's first operation was running smoothly.

Their mission was clear. The plan was to attend a gathering in which the public would be invited to ask Einstein questions. Nicholas would then ask a question while Serena hung back, stepping in only if necessary. They fully expected to be in and out of there in under an hour.

3

He sneered as he listened to the recording one last time.

"Ms. Wilcox, people say that your ideas are crazy and will never work. Let me tell you about crazy. I've witnessed that 'crazy' works, particularly when there's nothing left to lose, and when no one else has any other ideas. And I believe that's the position we're in. It's that person willing to lay everything on the table who makes a difference. You have moxie and crazy in near equal proportion."

He cackled even though he was alone. Serena Wilcox was an imbecile. Buick's modifiers of "crazy" and "moxie" were laughable; Serena wasn't cute and funny, like a puppy. She was a rodent, the first of an infestation yet to come. It was time to say goodbye to Serena Wilcox and to the Gödel Solution Institute.

If only he could. His hands were tied by the laws of the universe. It was infuriating that she was in his way, but that didn't mean that all was lost, not by a longshot. At the very least, containment was an option. He imagined the child-sized pony-tailed girl-woman in containment and he grinned. She'd be trapped like a trinket in a plastic egg in the antique coin toy dispensers he'd seen in a collector's database. And she'd never stop talking, not even then, he ruminated.

Yes, containing Serena Wilcox pleased him, but doing this lawfully was a different matter. In his day, technology had progressed to the point where isolation of time was now possible, that wasn't the issue. They could isolate or "contain" pockets of time, called Time Units. He was no scientist, but he understood the concept to mean that they could freeze, or perhaps more accurately "hold", Time Units. This technology was highly regulated, which was problematic.

The intention behind containment was that isolating time afforded researchers and investigators an opportunity to study the impact on the universe if the targeted event was manipulated. If a time curve event was changed, or even removed from the Time Unit entirely, there were always unintended circumstances. The review and analysis process always revolved around this question: will intervention cause more harm than good, or is the anticipated collateral damage an acceptable sacrifice for the greater good? Decisions often took several months. However, while a person or event was held in containment, the Time Unit was temporarily frozen for study, meaning that the data was removed from time travel access. It was as if the person or event didn't exist. The thought of Serena Wilcox's existence scrubbed from the universe cheered him immensely.

Unfortunately during the containment period the Time Unit was protected from modification until such time as the World Order decided what should be done with it, so unless he found a way to infiltrate the security system, he couldn't take Serena out of play. On the up side, containment meant that time travelers couldn't go there. No one could go in or out of the Time Unit. He would be free of Serena Wilcox for the duration of the containment.

The downside to this plan was that the longer the containment, the more risk that other time travelers across the curve will take notice. He didn't need more of Serena's kind nosing about his business. While she was a pesky flea, she was certainly not a physical threat. He was wary of travelers who might be sent in to investigate her disappearance. They would come armed with their unsophisticated weapons. Of course his own team could quickly overwhelm any primitive army sent to fetch Serena, that wasn't the point. The point was that he'd probably lose a few good men in the process. The idea of death by Tinker Toy was ludicrous! He respected his team more than that, even though he couldn't say the same about their respect for him.

Another negative he considered was that containment was strictly regulated and recorded. Therefore, the authority to manipulate or remove a Time Unit was typically denied, and already had been. His first request to remove Serena Wilcox from the playing field had been denied—no surprise there. The agency had initially agreed that removing Serena would cripple the Gödel Solution Institute and meet operation objectives. Then they reversed their decision and declined his request for Time Unit removal. They gave no explanation for their reversal. Instead, they had ordered a full analysis of what removing Serena Wilcox would do to the time curve.

He kept his rebuttal to himself as it would be career suicide to balk. Privately, he fumed. How could it be even *remotely* possible that removing Serena Wilcox would be worse than leaving her in play? She was the sole reason why he was stalled out in his mission. He was beyond frustrated, but what could he do? He was already working outside of the law as much as he dared.

The politics of the day had won out. Even though it was obvious that Time Unit containment was necessary, he was left waiting for approval. Meanwhile one conflict after another mounted up and with each new conflict Serena Wilcox burrowed further under his skin. She was the boil that he couldn't lance. It amused him that she called him the devil—if she only knew how little power he actually had. He was a minion at best.

Time travel was a significant military asset and everyone knew it. His expertise was required. So why tie his hands? Why did he have to beg for the World Order to let him do his job? He was the most experienced time-travel agent, he was the right-hand man for the highest ranking general of the RR Division of the World Order Armed Forces, and he was the most decorated spy in history. But what difference did any of this make if bureaucrats rendered him impotent?

To add insult to injury, the "RR" in the RR Division stood for Ruby Red. The division had been named in tribute to the pioneering days of time travel, when Serena Wilcox was at the helm. This bit of trivia enraged him, but the division dismissed his petition for a division name change without hearing him. He was slow to realize that while his position gave him the authority to tell his men to retreat, stay, or open fire, he was merely a pawn in a political chess game.

His team knew this too. The RR soldiers under his command resented that he held their lives in his hands even though he had never served in the military and, worst of all, that he was a spy. Political appointments had become commonplace in the military and routinely came down from the World Order, giving them no higher authority to appeal to.

Even though there had been multiple scandals involving faulty intelligence that had resulted in the deaths of troops, the political machine churned on. The military community and much of the general public doubted the steady stream of rulings that had cleared politicians and intelligence officers without a single indictment, regardless of much evidence to the contrary. Witnesses had had a way of dying in "accidents". Those who had made it to the stand had been discredited. The World Order had used propaganda to keep their narrative flowing. They had shifted the blame wholly onto the intelligence community. Spies were now despised and mistrusted more than tax collectors.

Regardless of what had really transpired, he had had nothing to do with any of those scandals. Nonetheless, his team believed that all spies had carried out the reprehensible policies that had left soldiers behind. He had learned early on to watch his back. Occasionally one of his men brushed up against him in the corridor. He knew that the rough physical contact was deliberate.

Normally he had nothing to do with the soldiers, as their functions were distinctly separate from his agenda and because they worked for different government agencies, so it didn't bother him much that his team didn't hold him in high esteem. He had been assigned to the RR division solely to lead them in and out of the time curve. His job was to manage the intricacies of time travel which included constant surveillance on GSI and other time travel entities that GSI would later spawn. Basically anything that fell under time travel was his domain.

The RR's missions were largely unrelated to the technology of time travel, other than to use it as a means of transport. The RR deployed to battlegrounds of the past to train in real-time stimulation exercises. They had other missions as well, but those were classified beyond his security clearance. His involvement in the missions was restricted to navigating the time travel aspects, but he often overstepped his authority by acting as a general when no high ranking officer was present.

One of his roles for the division was to advise the troops on how to maneuver around the footprints of GSI. This role required that he deliver regular briefings to the troops. He even had to serve alongside them on occasion, which of course the troops resented. All of this led to the precarious position he now found himself in—he had to lead the RR from behind, lest he be shot by friendly fire.

Despite their differences, the RR did agree with him on one thing. It was absurd that they were forced to tiptoe around GSI's idiotic bumbling through the time curve. How could the World Order allow primitive and ignorant people of the past to interfere with the future? Politics! Their common enemies—GSI, Serena Wilcox, and the World Order—unified him with the RR in hate. Hatred was not enough to secure loyalty or respect, though. He knew that he was the fourth enemy on their list, coming in just after the World Order.

Sometimes the World Order wasn't cold, calculated, shrewd, evil, or power-grabbing. Sometimes they were simply incompetent. His current roadblock was in place because the WO couldn't agree on how to contain his requested Time Unit, when to contain it, or for how long. Some hold-outs even suggested that containment wasn't recommended. Instead of granting him his long overdue containment permit, he was advised to continue to "work around" GSI. That meant that he had to work around Serena Wilcox, the most irritating woman he had ever met. Of course that wasn't saying much. He knew so few women, and all of them had been from before his time. He was fairly sure that Serena was a representative of why the universe was better off without double X zygotes.

That was the problem with politicians. They spoke out of their backsides with no ground in reality. If they had worked even one day of an RR mission they would have seen that working around Serena Wilcox was intolerable. She was the cause of the scrapped Argonne Offensive testing site that had been in the making for years. All of those man hours scrapped in one day, because of a short middle-aged woman from the 2000's!

Nothing like that could ever happen now, and he couldn't fathom why they would put up with it bleeding on them from the past. Not only would they never allow stupid people, crazy people, or people with "moxie" to interfere with World Order initiatives, but it wouldn't even be possible today that a *woman* could stop up the works. Because, in his day, it was as it should have been all along.

The XX zygote was a thing of the past. No longer necessary for procreation, the decision to terminate them had been a nearly unanimous decision. In his time, and for all points on the time curve to follow, there was only one gender. Women didn't exist.

4

Ann Kinji looked up over her glasses at Serena, who had shown up unannounced and was standing in her office doorway. "What brings you here? I thought you were on your way to meet Albert Einstein?

"I have a few questions for you first."

"First of all, I can't guarantee any answers. Secondly, your timing couldn't be worse. There's a new development."

"What new development?" Serena glanced around Ann's office, noting the new aquarium full of exotic fish. Ann had apparently redecorated during the hiatus. "I like it."

Ann prompted, "What did you come in here for?"

"Something's been nagging at me. When Eduardo delivered his first board meeting for GSI, he mentioned that 1939 was farther back than we could currently time travel, but then he programmed me to go to Davenport, Iowa, 1939. Was this before or after the MOTF coerced him to extract data from the orphans? What I'm getting at is, was Eduardo giving us a clue when he specifically mentioned the connection between 1939 and the limits of the time window? Could I have known early on about the CIA's involvement and the MOTF if I'd been paying closer attention?"

Ann grabbed a pencil from the top drawer of her desk. A few weeks ago she had removed all pencils from her desktop as the first step toward breaking her habit of chewing on erasers when under stress. But earlier today she had dipped into her emergency stash of unsharpened number twos. "You know that I can't discuss Eduardo."

"He was giving us a clue back then, wasn't he? I'm kicking myself that I missed it."

Ann fiddled with one of the pencils from her stash. "You're good, but you're no mind reader. I don't fault you for not picking up on it. Eduardo could have read us in at any time and he chose not to. His loyalty was to the CIA then, although you bring up a good point. Apparently his loyalties were shifting. He must have been having doubts even before things went belly up."

"Why can't you tell me where Eduardo is? How can I do my job if you are holding back pieces of the puzzle?"

Ann bit the top of the eraser off completely. She spit it out and shot it whole into the trash container under her desk. "I can't tell you because I don't know."

Serena's eyes flew wide open. "Well, that's not good. How can this be over your head?"

Ann gestured for Serena to look around her office. "If you haven't already noticed, instead of the seal of the office of the President of the United States and a designer crew of Secret Service agents, my new décor involves only a coffee maker and a fish tank."

"But President Joe is your personal friend, as well as someone who respects you. You'll never really stop being President anyway—not where it counts. To be honest, we all think of you and President Joe as co-Presidents. If anything, you coach him through his presidency, making you still sort of the president, don't you agree? So why is he leaving you out like this?"

"For exactly the reason that you mentioned. It's absurd that I'm still involved in anything that goes on in the Cube. I'm no longer President and I shouldn't be acting like one. I'm not Joe's advisor. I'm not part of his cabinet. I have nothing to do with his administration. GSI and the executive branch of the United States government have nothing whatsoever to do with each other, other than cooperation between government agencies."

"All right, I do understand, but Eduardo is critical to GSI. Why is the government overstepping? You assured us that you were in full control of GSI. First it was a private institute and then you amended that status to tell us that GSI is a 'hybrid' of private and government, like a joint venture. But now? It looks to me as if the government has taken over. Am I working for you or for them? Am I a detective or a spy?"

Ann sighed. "Are you finished?"

Serena contemplated that question before concluding that she was indeed finished.

Ann tapped her eraser-less pencil on the edge of her desk a few times and then chucked the entire pencil into the trash. "This is out of my hands. Yes, you called it. Eduardo's absence has struck a heavy blow. But if you really want to help, the best thing you can do right now is your job. You pitched your Einstein idea and Buick signed off on it. What you're doing with that, I don't know, and I have bigger fish to fry. You do your job so that I can do mine."

"What is your bigger fish?"

Ann shook her head. "Not now."

"To be honest, I'm not optimistic that meeting Einstein will be of much use. Sometimes I blurt things out without thinking it through."

"Desperate ideas are all we've got right now. Go."

Serena held her ground. "You've always been an intimidating force. I can't imagine that anyone could push you out of GSI without a fight. How does 'the other guy' look?"

"No, you've got this wrong. I didn't fight against them, I fought *for* them. I told Joe that he needed to step up. As long as I was holding his hand through his presidency it was as if I had never left."

Serena squinted up her green eyes and clenched her jaw. The effect of this made her look like an angry elf. "But letting go of GSI doesn't make any sense, and it hurts all of us. I didn't sign on to be a spy."

"Again, you're misunderstanding the situation. I pushed Joe to take the reins, and he did. I'm proud of him for that. Unfortunately he underestimated how quickly this would spiral out of control."

Serena sank into a chair. Her short chat was more involved than she had expected it to be. She may as well have a seat, she told herself. When she saw the scornful expression on Ann's face she stood back up.

Ann pointed to the door, but Serena lingered. "Are you saying that the president doesn't know where Eduardo is either? How could he have lost sight of him, and how could you have? You're right Ann, I don't understand."

Ann leaned across her desk and lowered her voice. "Eduardo has entered the witness relocation program."

The light finally dawned for Serena. "Oh! He's been threatened? Who's after him? If it's the MOTF, you can't hide him. They'll find him wherever you've put him."

Ann leapt out of her chair, sending it flying backward beyond the chair mat. She left the chair where it landed. She paced her office perimeter as she spoke. "Joe put the MOTF on the terrorist watch list and assigned a special task force to follow their tracks. He wanted to know everywhere that the Red-headed Devil had been, how many others were with him, and of course if any of them were still here. And before you get bent out of shape, no, you didn't need to know any of this. This is a military intelligence operation, and far removed from what you do."

"Can you tell me what they discovered? Are they still here?"

Ann stopped pacing. She said nothing for several seconds. "No, I can't tell you anything. I can't tell you anything because I don't know anything. They are all gone."

"The MOTF are gone?"

Ann locked eyes with Serena. "No. The entire Special Forces team is gone."

Serena let that information settle in. "I understand now why you're worried that Eduardo will be next, but what makes you think that anyone can hide him from the MOTF?"

"I don't. It was a decision that was made and I've chosen to respect that decision."

"Why not let him continue to work for GSI under our protection? Eduardo isn't safe anywhere. All witness protection is doing is holding us back from getting the help that we need."

Ann resumed her pacing. "Joe was horrified when his Special Forces team vanished, but his immediate response was to replace them with a new team, whose mission was to find out what happened to the first team. The first thing that the new team did is squirrel Eduardo away, under Joe's command. I respect that decision even if I don't agree with it."

"We aren't getting Eduardo back is what you're saying."

"That's what I'm saying."

Serena frowned. "The risk factor has shot way up without Eduardo."

Ann scoffed. "Since when are you concerned about risk?"

"And another thing: I don't like the idea of two separate investigations going on at the same time. I don't see how we can avoid getting into each other's way. The government has already caused us a huge headache when they took our best person from us, pointlessly I have to say. If the MOTF want Eduardo, they'll find him. None of this makes any sense. Does Agent Estep know about this?"

Ann looked away.

Serena whistled through her teeth, or at least she would have if she knew how to whistle. The sound was more of a sigh. "He's leading the replacement team, isn't he?"

Ann rolled her chair back into its position on the mat. "Yes."

"Then Estep knows where Eduardo is!"

Ann reached out and grabbed Serena's arm by the wrist. "Let this go."

Serena's eyebrows shot up. "What else aren't you telling me?"

Ann hesitated.

"Let me help," Serena pleaded.

Ann said nothing.

Serena waited as one minute passed and then two, but Ann seemed unwilling to budge. She was about to give up when Ann said something that she couldn't quite hear.

Ann repeated what she had said. "The new team is missing too."

Serena's asked the question even though she had a sinking feeling that she already knew the answer. "Agent Estep?"

Ann shook her head slowly. "Gone."

5

Mandolin should have been surprised to get a call from Serena Wilcox but he wasn't. Somehow he had a feeling that he would be called into GSI any day now. He wasn't accustomed to being on the right side of the law. When agents came around to pick him up, he half expected one of them to push his head down while helping him into the government vehicle.

Mandolin rode in comfort and style to GSI's headquarters. This was a far cry from his previous ride to the institute when he was brought in for questioning. He felt freer without cuffs on his wrists, but it was the new respect the agents gave him that overwhelmed him. I could get used to this, he thought. Mandolin's esteem soared even higher after his arrival at GSI.

Serena greeted him with a warm handshake and four words. "I need your help."

Serena's words were a balm to his soul. Since when did anyone ask for Mandolin? Since when did he matter to anyone? He had never achieved his dream of becoming a Marine, or even his expectation of becoming a law-abiding citizen, but he believed in second chances. This was his. Aloud, Mandolin only grunted.

Serena explained, "I need for you to help me find Agent Estep and his team. I must warn you, this could be dangerous. In fact, it probably *is* dangerous. Yes, I think we can assume that there is a risk involved. Now that I think about it, it's pretty much a safe bet…"

Mandolin cut her off. "I can handle it."

Serena lightly touched Mandolin's muscular arm. When he flinched she let go. "Mandolin, I'm trying to say that this mission goes above and beyond what anyone should require you to do, regardless of your plea bargain or whatever it is that you've bound yourself to. This mission could cost you your life. Nobody should be forced into this type of situation. I'm rethinking this whole thing. Asking you to do it is taking advantage of your situation."

Mandolin shrugged. "Every day could cost me my life."

"Are you sure you want to do this? If you have any doubts, say so. I don't have the authority to force you to do this and I wouldn't do that to you anyway."

"No doubts. Tell me what to do."

"I need you to time travel with me."

Mandolin's belly laugh made his whole body shake. In a man of his size, the effect was spectacular.

His laugh was infectious and Serena succumbed to it for a few seconds. Then she forced her face into a sober expression. "I'm serious."

"You don't think they'll notice a man with my good looks?" Mandolin flashed two gold teeth and flexed his bronze tattooed biceps.

Serena chuckled. "We'll hide you."

"I can't help you from a hidey hole."

"Just lie low unless we need you. If we need you, be a pit bull for us. Got it?"

"Ready when you are."

"I was born ready." Serena smiled.

Mandolin winked and followed her to the launch pad. He allowed the crew to fuss around him, soaking up every minute of this attention. Someone snapped a time travel band on his wrist, another gave him a satchel of supplies, and the third filled his ear with instructions. Mandolin caught hardly any of it.

At this same hour Nicholas was also being fitted with time travel gear. He was relieved that his participation in the mission hadn't been cancelled. His role had been in jeopardy after Serena became aware that the level of danger had risen. Some had questioned the wisdom of involving a minor in a hazardous operation. But Nicholas had persuaded GSI to keep him on. He argued that he was of age to join the military with a parental waiver, and his parents had already signed the waiver for this mission. Why should he be barred from service to his country through time travel, when he would have been allowed to march directly into combat if he had wanted to? No one could refute that logic.

They wouldn't all fit in the time machine so wristbands were the way to go. Besides, it was difficult to hide Ruby Red and Serena was weary of corn fields. Regardless of the valid reasons for leaving Ruby Red on the tarmac, it was with reluctance that she abandoned her custom made time machine, especially since it was raining. She idly wondered if anyone had remembered to water the flowers that the crew had planted for her in the portal. She resigned herself to the probability that the flowers were long dead.

Beav interrupted Serena's brooding. "Are you sure you won't wait until we can give you a new security team?"

Mandolin snorted. "If you wanted more guns, you should have told me. One call, my posse is here."

Serena shook her head. "We're not going to start a war. I just want a bodyguard. I need only one guy for that."

The plan to meet Einstein was still on, but Serena had a strong feeling that she would run into the MOTF as well. She realized how little she had thought this through. Maybe she did need an army.

She thought about her conversation with Ann. She tried to guess the MOTF's motivations for snatching GSI's Special Forces teams. The most logical reason she could come up with was leverage. She had a hunch that they'd offer to return their teams if GSI agreed to stay out of their way. Wasn't that what the MOTF wanted?

75

She couldn't think of anything else they'd need from GSI other than to be left alone to do whatever it is they were doing, unhindered.

Also, because Estep had messed up the MOTF's assignment in the Argonne Forest he hadn't made himself popular. She figured that some of this was payback; revenge, making a point, and warning GSI to stay out of their way. The good news was that this meant that their teams were likely alive and well, held up somewhere until the MOTF were ready to state their demands.

Serena had no intention of staying out of the MOTF's way. She anticipated that an encounter with the Red Headed Devil wouldn't go well. But she had Mandolin to help her escape, assuming that the MOTF weren't allowed to zap her, vaporize her, or whatever it is that they did to people to erase them. Her imagination conjured up futuristic weapons with electronic sound effects and flashing lights.

Serena was banking on the idea that the MOTF were just as bound to the laws of the universe as they were. If GSI was forced to tread lightly when it came to altering the course of history, wouldn't the same be true for the MOTF? In this way, Serena felt as if she was invincible. How could the MOTF kill her without threatening their *own* time window? No, she didn't think she was in any danger beyond what Mandolin could handle.

Serena's thoughts kept her quiet for several seconds. Mandolin and Nicholas waited patiently for her to tell them what to do. Beav said, "If you're going to stand around, at least go back inside. You're going to be soaked to the gills."

"No, no. I'm good." Serena waved to Beav before giving Mandolin and Nicholas the green light. Within seconds the three of them were blinking in the sunlight of a beautiful day. She spoke quickly, in case her arrival was expected. "Mandolin, see that clump of trees over there? I want you to hunker down and hide in the woods. Your wrist band is on vibrate mode. Don't turn on the lights or sound features, just in case."

Mandolin chuckled. "You think I know how to use this thing? Whatever you did to it is how it's going to stay."

Serena said, "Find me when it signals you."

"And how will I know where you are?"

Nicholas grabbed Mandolin's wristband and twisted it around to show him the underside of the band. "There's a GPS locator on it. We've got you on a split screen. This is you, and this is Ms. Wilcox. Right now you see that the coordinates are almost identical because you're standing right next to each other."

Mandolin squinted at the tiny display. "I don't do GPS. It'll send me over a cliff."

Nicholas shrugged. "You'll need to use the audio function then. Here, put this in your ear." He gave Mandolin a nearly invisible earpiece. He leaned into Mandolin's personal space bubble to adjust the band. "There. Now you'll hear directions every time Serena takes a step."

Mandolin and Nicholas stared at Serena. She stared back at them. "Oh, right." She walked a few feet away and then returned to where she was.

A digitized female voice told him where Serena was, step by step, even to the point of telling him what the surroundings looked like from her point of view. Mandolin snorted. "That'll do." He was blown away by this technology, but he still didn't trust it. What Serena didn't know was that he had no intention of staying in the woods anyway. He knew how to follow someone without being seen. He bid Serena and Nicholas adieu and pretended to hunker down into his hiding place.

6

Serena figured that 1915 was a good year to approach Einstein with time travel related questions. It was the year before the publication of his paper on the theory of relativity. Einstein had presented a series of lectures to the Prussian Academy of Sciences in Berlin, otherwise known as the Preußische Akademie der Wissenschaften. It was there that Einstein introduced the equation that replaced Newton's law of gravity, Einstein's Field Equations. This was one of the defining moments of his career. What better time to talk Einstein than when he was at his peak, in the last lecture of his series in November 1915?

"Ms. Wilcox, why did you change your mind about talking to Einstein? You told me that it could alter history if we interacted with him."

"Nicholas, history has already been manipulated by the MOTF. All bets are off. Besides, I trust that we can pull off our cover story. We have no intention of interfering with history."

"Your use of the word 'intention' is suspect," Nicholas said without jest.

"How old are you, Nicholas? Sixteen or sixty?" Serena laughed.

"I take a more serious view of this than you do."

Serena attempted to give Nicholas a playful fist bump but he didn't respond.

"You take a more serious view of everything than I do."

The pair walked together in silence, the tall lanky boy alongside the short middle-aged woman. They looked to passerby to be mother and son—nothing out of the ordinary. Their period piece clothing had been customized to the smallest detail. They fit right in.

The GSI production team had learned that it was faster to create handcrafted replicas of period piece items and clothing than it was for them to find what they were looking for in antique stores, even if online. It was best to keep their production needs in house anyway. Beav realized that this presented a bigger challenge than even he could make time for.

The need for seamstresses and costume designers led GSI to recruit from the entertainment and fashion industries. Although designers weren't allowed in secured areas on the GSI campus, they went through a vetting process and were required to sign a non-disclosure agreement.

Despite these security procedures their presence at GSI was disruptive. The fashion industry attracted the attention of tabloid photojournalists and videographers. They also had their own ideas about what Beav's team should do. To complete Serena's image, several designers had insisted that they give her a makeover.

Serena submitted to having her hair done in an Edwardian hairstyle, a popular do from 1915. Her long dark hair was perfect for the sweeping up-to of the Edwardian. Her hair was first wound in a variation of a simple bun, an uneventful sight so far. It wasn't until the stylist worked on the billowy top that the team gathered around to watch. The effect was startling. Serena's hair had been swept off of her face into a pompadour, a dramatic halo of hair over her elfin face.

Serena strode the streets of 1915 like a peacock, her hair making her appear to be several inches taller than her usual ground-hugging self. Taller, but still not tall, she glanced up at Nicholas. "Try to enjoy this. It isn't every day that you get to meet Albert Einstein."

Finding Einstein wouldn't be challenging because they knew when and where his next public appearance would be held. What could throw a wrench in their plans was the possibility that Einstein wouldn't take Nicholas' question. What would they do then? Their cover story could fall apart if they had to resort to more aggressive measures to pin Einstein down, and Serena realized that their cover story wasn't going to work as well as she had expected anyway. What she hadn't thought about was the fact that she was a woman in 1915.

As she watched one male figure after another pass them on their way to the lecture, she saw not a single woman among them. She also saw no young people. The college student identity wasn't going to work for them this time around.

Nicholas brought up another potential pitfall. "I read that Einstein was stopped on the street by people wanting him to explain 'that theory'. He'd tell them, 'Pardon me, sorry! Always I am mistaken for Professor Einstein.' What if he does that to us?"

"If we throw him off guard he'll be flustered. He might not fend us off. Let's try it now."

Nicholas shook his head. "But I just told you, his response to strangers approaching him on the street is to blow them off."

"Before the lecture he'll be keyed up," Serena grabbed Nicholas by his sleeve. "I see him now. He's about to go in."

Nicholas protested, "We have no cover story."

"Spontaneity is the mother of all invention." Serena tugged at his sleeve, attempting to steer him toward Einstein.

"Don't you mean 'Necessity is the mother of all invention'?"

"They mean the same thing. Let's go!"

Nicholas hastened his pace but was still mulling over what she had said. "I don't think they're the same thing, Ms. Wilcox. And let go of me." He shrugged her hand off his sleeve.

"They are now. Come on! He's going in, we have to catch him!" She raced ahead, but not for long.

Nicholas zipped through the gaggle of men in suits that trudged forward up the steps. He appeared beside Albert Einstein

87

as if by teleportation. Serena stood back, stunned and out of breath, way behind and already lost in the crowed. Einstein, startled by the young man who seemed to pop in out of nowhere, displayed a shocked expression like a caricature. So he really looked like that, Nicholas thought.

Before Einstein had regained his composure Nicholas blurted, "Can warped spacetime, your theory of gravity, um, can it be made a different way? Could God have made the world in a different way?"

Einstein muttered, "Whether the necessity of logical simplicity leaves any freedom at all. This I have said."

"Yes, I know. I read it. I mean, I, never mind. If the future is changed, will the world be remade? Or will it remain constant except for the chain of events directly affected? Like if one person went, um, missing, would the whole world change?"

Einstein peered up at Nicholas. "God does not play dice." He viewed the boy with clinical observation. His conclusion ended with "Hmph."

Nicholas looked furtively around him for Serena. "You know I'm not from, um, here?"

Einstein nodded slowly. For a moment his stress-induced stomach pains were forgotten. His wispy hair floated serenely in the autumn air. His eyes were warm, friendly and full of intimacy. "God is not malicious."

Nicholas said, "If the future were to be changed, God would make sure that nothing bad happens? So it would all stay on course even if we, if someone, had to do something to stop someone or something bad from happening?"

Einstein's youthful countenance and ever-present slight smile belied the gravity of his words. "Do what you must."

89

And with those final words, the conversation was over. Einstein entered the building amid a small crowd. No one had overheard their conversation, although several had tried. Nicholas watched Einstein until he could no longer see him. Then he made his way back down the steps to where Serena was waiting.

She said, "Well? What did he say?"

"You're good to go, Ms. Wilcox. He said to do what we need to do. Apparently the world won't implode. What do you plan to do anyway?"

"I don't know yet. Right now we need to hurry back to where we left Mandolin and get ourselves home. It's getting dark already."

"We'll make it. It's not far."

Serena grinned. "I can't believe you got the answer to my question from Albert Einstein himself!"

The two were patting themselves on the back for a job well done as they rounded the corner of the Prussian Academy of Sciences building. It was there that they were jostled by a gaggle of passerby. The gaggle didn't clear up as they moved along, but instead drew in closer, trapping them with their body mass. They moved together this way down the city block until the grey-suited mob steered them into an alley.

Once deep inside the alley, they were obscured from the street. One of the men grabbed Serena while another man shoved Nicholas outside of the mob. The entire clutch including Serena disappeared. Only Nicholas remained in the dark alley.

Before Nicholas could decide what to do, Mandolin appeared. "We can't stay here."

Nicholas was frozen.

"Come on, move!" Mandolin grabbed Nicholas' wrist to activate his time travel band. Mandolin arrived safely on the GSI tarmac with Nicholas at his side.

Beav asked, "Where's Serena?"

Mandolin shook his head and requested to talk to Ann Kinji. Beav brought him into her office and stayed to listen. Mandolin could barely look Ann in the eye when he told her what happened. His first mission as Serena's bodyguard couldn't have been a more miserable failure.

7

Agent Estep glared at the MOTF. "How long will you detain us? You can't keep us here indefinitely. If you planned to kill us you would have done it by now."

One of them answered, "Termination has not been ruled out."

Estep scoffed. "Bull. Tell me what's going on."

A burst of activity distracted the three MOTF who guarded him. Estep, bound by

93

chains to a metal framed guillotine, craned his neck to see the source of the commotion. He moaned. "That's about my luck. They've sent me Pippi Shortsocks."

"Happy to see you too, Estep. And you're welcome for finding and saving your donkey behind." Serena grinned.

Estep said, "Don't need both words, one or the other will do. Either donkey or… Forget it. Saving me? How? What did you do, make a deal with the Devil?"

"Yes, I did. All they want is a sit down. I've agreed to talk with them, and they've agreed to let you and the Special Forces teams go."

One of the guards released Estep's chains by directing a sensor at the latch. Estep stood, stretched, and groaned. "This is going to hurt tomorrow." He surveyed the room.

Serena noticed the expression on his face. She whispered, "Whatever you're thinking about doing—don't."

Estep grunted, "I can't leave you here."

"Yes, you can. They won't hurt me. Taking me out of play isn't in their best interests. For whatever reason, they need me to stay alive and live out my life. Trust me, they won't touch a hair on my head. I'm apparently important to their future, and to yours." She smirked.

Estep sighed. "What will it take to get you to stop gloating?"

"How many times did you complain about having to, how did you put it, 'find Serena Waldo' and save me? Add it up, buddy boy. I owe you that many rounds of gloating."

Estep hugged her. The action was brisk and brief, but it shocked them both.

He mumbled, "Thanks for saving my 'arse'."

Serena added, "Well, this is awkward. I don't know what to say when you're being nice to me."

Estep pointed at the door. "Not a problem, they're taking me now." Two of the guards escorted Estep out. Everyone else was rounded up as well. When every member of both teams of Special Forces was accounted for they were promptly sent back to their present time. Only Serena Wilcox was left behind in the year 2082.

She hadn't seen much of the future yet, only the holding room where she was waiting for the Redheaded Devil to arrive. But she certainly had had an eyeful already. "Why do all of you look exactly alike?" she asked one of the guards.

"Evolution."

"What do you mean by that?" she pressed. Serena coached herself to extract as much information about them as she could.

"We evolved into a humanity that is devoid of racism and bigotry."

"But you're all white!" Had they committed genocide on a scale so massive that the world would never recover? She felt dizzy.

The guard snapped. "We are not white! We have no pigmentation. There is no color, that's the point."

"You're all albino then? You've caused a mutation of a recessive gene or something?"

"No! We are not albino. We have no pigmentation. Take note of the darkness of my eyes."

Serena shivered. "Your eyes are so black that they look like one big pupil."

The guard's face screwed up into an angry wad. "Eye color indicates rank."

"So you're born with a rank, like a class system?"

The guard refuted, "We earn rank. Eye color is changed upon promotion. We have no division, no bigotry, no bias, and no classism. We have evolved into the perfect human race."

"Is that what the red hair is about too? Rank? Only your leader has red hair."

"Something like that, yes."

"You haven't convinced me that 'no pigmentation' is a good thing, not at all. I find it hateful actually, and the very definition of racism. The goal has always been to accept differences, not make all of us the same."

The guard leered at her.

"Why are you looking at me that way?" Serena felt a crawling sensation on her skin. She reminded herself that they couldn't hurt her.

"Besides racism, we rid humanity of misogyny."

"Of…" Serena gasped. "By doing what? Are you telling me that there are no women?"

The guard stared at her. "You validate why we made the change to a one-gendered society. The double X made humanity feeble."

Serena swallowed past the lump in her throat. "It's hard to move on from this, but I must ask, if there are no women, does that mean that you killed them all? Did you take their eggs first? How else would you procreate?"

"First, yes, we vaporized the women. It was a humane kill, quick and painless. Secondly, we have no use for women; I thought I made that clear. We clone when we need to refresh our population."

"So every baby is born in an artificial uterus I assume? Born colorless and male?"

The other two guards snickered. They had been eavesdropping on the conversation but had chosen to stay out of it. The guard she was speaking with said, "Your ignorance is astounding. We clone adults."

"You are like robots then?" Serena blinked.

"I didn't say that we didn't have partners or domiciles. Society functions better when the young are independent and the old are disposed of before dependency sets in."

Serena fought against the surge of nausea swelling up inside of her. She refused to give them the satisfaction of watching her retch. "You haven't rid yourselves of hate by disposing of women and races and babies and children. You've made everyone the same by stripping away all that is unique about humanity. But you didn't strip away the hate! You left it to fester, and become stronger. Stripping away the beauty of diversity has left you laid bare. Your hatred has found a new way to flourish."

The Redheaded Devil waltzed into the holding room as Serena finished her impromptu speech. He clapped slowly, one infuriating clap at a time. He drawled, "Clever. Astute. Poetic, while a bit trite. Probably true. Don't care."

Serena dug her fingernails into the palm of her hand, willing herself not to lose control. She asked, "Why did you want to talk to me?"

"You've become a thorn in my side. I want to eradicate you, but alas, my hands are tied at the moment. I am asking you politely to stay out of my business."

"And if I don't?"

The Devil flicked out his forked tongue and hissed. "I'll find you."

Serena startled him by changing the subject. "Why do you have a forked tongue? This has been bugging me ever since I saw it."

"Does my tongue scare you?" He drew Serena close to him and flicked his tongue near her face. Then he released her, threw his head back, and cackled. "I already told you that I'm not the Devil, and yet you insist on referring to me as 'The Redheaded Devil'."

Serena's mouth was a silent "O". She recovered and forced her voice to remain steady. "You're listening to us?"

"You're half right."

"So you're watching us too then."

"You saw how easily I snatched your entire security team, and then your *replacement* security team. No matter how many teams you pile on, I'll round them all up."

"Why are you doing this?"

"All you need to know is that I'm always watching, always listening. You can think about that when you put on your floral nightie with the blue buttons and snuggle in close to your daft husband. You can contemplate it when you tuck in your genetically challenged children at night, all three destined to grow up to be as bland as you are. You can think about it when you're in the shower, lathering up with your sulfate-free shampoo and shaving with your pink razor, the one you keep next to that ceramic soap dish. And when you look in the chipped mirror beside your medicine cabinet at night that's when, Serena," he hissed as he unrolled his tongue, "is when you'll see my face!"

He loomed over her and just when she was certain that he was going to

103

strangle her, he zapped her out of the holding room in 2082 and back to present day.

She materialized on the GSI launching pad as if she were thrown roughly on the ground. She stood up on her wobbly legs and leaned over. All of the fear that she had been holding inside her bubbled up. She vomited again and again until there was nothing left.

8

Ann didn't look up from her desk when she said, "The architect should have put in a revolving door."

Already gathered in her office were Agent Estep, Beav, Lehman, Nicholas and Mandolin. None of them greeted the sixth person who entered the room—they simply stared at her, shocked by her appearance. Finally the quiet became loud enough that Ann looked up.

105

"Serena, you're back!" She raced upon her tiny pretty feet to meet her. She stopped short. "You're white as a sheet!"

Serena gasped. Then she broke down into a torrent of racking sobs.

Ann exchanged a quizzical glance with Lehman. "Do you know what this is about? Did they hurt her?" Her confusion morphed into anger. "Did any of you see her before now? Why didn't anyone tell me that she was back?"

Beav clapped a hand on Ann's shoulder. He lowered his voice. "This is the first we've seen her."

Serena's breakdown was too much for Agent Estep. He slipped out the door, even though it meant squeezing past Serena who hadn't budged from the doorway. He couldn't get through so he moved her out of the way. She didn't even notice that her feet had momentarily been lifted off the ground.

Estep stayed away until he thought it was safe to return. He'd had experience with this sort of thing, having lived in a house full of sisters. When he made it back Serena's tears were exhausted. All that remained were gasps, shudders, sniffles and a puffy blotchy face.

He handed her a coffee loaded with cream and sugar, just the way she liked it. "You got me coffee?" She laughed, choked, and blew her nose. "You must really think you owe me one."

"I thought you could use a cup, that's all."

Ann instructed them to sit. She waited until they were settled before she perched on top of her desk, a vantage point that looked down upon everyone else. No one knew if the diminutive Japanese-American's habit of physically upstaging people was deliberate, but it was certainly effective. They looked at her expectantly.

107

She said, "You were about to tell me why Serena is missing. Now she's obviously here. When she's composed herself she can tell us what happened." Serena shook her head. Ann pointed at Nicholas. "You first, then you can go." She glowered at Beav. "You should know by now that I don't like youth involved in these things. He's here now, what can we do? Go ahead Nicholas."

Nicholas stammered. They strained their ears to hear him. "I, um, I asked Albert Einstein the questions and he answered. Then I told Ms. Wilcox what he said and we were walking away from the building. Suddenly we were overtaken by men in suits who pushed us into a traveling mosh pit. They carried us into the alley. Then they took off with Ms. Wilcox and left me there all by myself. Then Mr. Mandolin came and he brought me back."

Ann nodded. "Are you getting all of this Lehman?"

Lehman nodded. He had been recording the session, anticipating that Ann would want a record of every word said.

The heels of Ann's shoes clicked on the side of the desk as she swung them in rhythm with her thoughts. "Nicholas, did you tell Serena everything that Einstein said to you?"

"Yes, Madam President."

"I'm not—never mind, thank you. You may go. Your parents are waiting for you in the lobby, are they not?" Ann waved for Beav to escort Nicholas out. After the two had left the office she called after Beav, "If you see Buick out there, send him in."

Beav popped his head back in the door and gave her his two-fingered salute. "Will do."

Nicholas' parents were engaged in animated conversation with secretary Ruby. Beav was able to drop off his charge and slip back out of the lobby without delay. He caught another lucky break when he saw Buick coming out of his office at that very moment. He snagged him and headed back to Ann's door.

In total, Beav was gone for only three minutes, but it felt like much longer. They had sat in silence while waiting for his return. After Buick took the chair that Nicholas had vacated, everyone stared at Serena. She felt the weight of their gaze. "I can talk now. I'll start with what happened during the mission.

It was a success, as far as that goes. I got what I wanted out of it. Einstein answered Nicholas with philosophical riddles, but the meaning was unmistakable. He told Nicholas that we should do what needs to be done."

Ann summarized. "We can take the MOTF out without catastrophic results."

"Yes, that's what I got out of it. I don't see any reason why we should hold back. I've seen the future and it's not pretty." Serena stirred her coffee with a plastic spoon and then studied the resulting swirls.

When it was obvious that the briefing had stalled out, Lehman paused the recording and closed his eyes for a few minutes. The team counted ceiling tiles, plucked at hangnails, doodled, checked text messages, and played games on their phones. Finally Ann resumed the briefing. Lehman released the system from pause mode and resigned himself to a long night.

Ann said, "I want to hear from Mandolin."

Mandolin sat up straighter in his chair.

She said, "I want your take on this. What did you think of the MOTF?"

Mandolin frowned. "I don't understand the question."

"You referred to the man you met as the Devil. When you saw the people who presumably work for him, what did you think?"

"Demons in suits."

She pressed, "You have described the MOTF as evil, that's clear. Is it possible that you are mistaken? Could it be that they are studying us? They haven't hurt any of you. What I'm saying is, impressions and perceptions can be wrong. Is it possible that you've made a mistake?"

Mandolin fixed his dark eyes on Ann. "My only mistake is that I didn't get there fast enough."

Ann followed up. "Had you been there sooner, you would have attempted to physically prevent the MOTF from taking Serena?"

Mandolin snorted. "Not 'attempt'."

Ann slid across her desk until she could reach her top drawer. She pulled out a pencil. Everyone cringed, expecting her to bite the eraser. They relaxed when they saw that she was content to tap the pencil on her hand to punctuate her words. "There's nothing you could have done. You got Nicholas back here and you reported what happened. I'm more than satisfied with your work on this mission. I want you to stay on."

Mandolin stumbled over his words but he managed to say, "It would be my honor." He marveled at how many second chances he was getting. But this could be his last second chance. If he screwed up again he was out for sure, he told himself.

Ann pointed at the door with her pencil. "Get some sleep. I'll need you back in a few hours."

Mandolin tried to comply but he couldn't get out of his chair. The seat wasn't designed for people his size. He finally wriggled free after a few astonishing contortions. He left the office, his empty chair spinning.

Ann said, "I'm not convinced that we can declare war on the MOTF. I'm telling you to convince me. What makes them evil?" No one said anything. "It's not that I don't believe you, but I need something more to give to the president and congress. We're involving the armed forces. We need more. I won't call President Joe until you convince me of a clear and present danger."

Beav said, "I agree. I personally am not willing to support this plan without some sort of official justification and documentation. Buick is here now. Mandolin and Nicholas are out of the room. In other words, the core team is accounted for and no one's here who shouldn't be. Lehman is recording the session—we're ready. There's no time like the present to hear what happened to Serena."

The only sound was the tapping of Ann's pencil. Beav turned toward Serena. "I've never seen you break down like what we witnessed a few minutes ago. So are you going to take a stab at that elephant in the room? If not you, Estep was there. One of you—start talking." Estep and Serena looked at each other. "Come on, you're both professionals, right? Pull yourselves together. No more delays."

No one spoke for several long seconds. Finally Estep said, "I don't know what happened to her. She's the only one who can answer that."

Serena steadied herself. She rubbed her hands together and then folded them. She was reminded of a finger play that her mother taught her when she was little. "Here's the church and here's the steeple,

115

open it up and see all the people." The next line involved keeping the fingers on the outside of the closed fist. "Here's the church and here's the steeple, open it up. Where're all the people?" Yes, where're all the people?

Estep abruptly got up and snapped his fingers directly in front of Serena's face with an ear-cracking pop. "Snap out of it! You're bigger than they are. Don't let them beat you down." Then he took his seat while the rest of them held their breath.

Serena blinked a few times but Estep's medicine worked magic. She started talking and didn't stop for a good solid hour.

9

Serena spoke without interruption. She paused only briefly to swallow a sip of now-cold coffee and gather her thoughts for the next round. Lehman monitored communications from her first sentence to her last. When Serena's speech veered into intensely personal tangents he contemplated whether or not he should cease recording. He decided that if the world were to one day analyze the pioneering days of time travel technology, full disclosure and the raw truth was best. He'd leave it to someone else to edit the material.

Serena maintained little eye contact while she spoke, which was uncharacteristic for her. Her speech had a halting start and her voice trailed off from time to time, but no one complained. This was the one time when everyone let her talk for as long as it took.

"I don't even know where to begin. I guess I should start with what happened when I was snatched in the alley after seeing Einstein. I was in the alley one second and in the future the next.

"I was brought into an upscale office. Let me describe it to you. There was a glut of indulgences on display. I saw fine wines, not that I really know anything about wines, but even I could tell that these bottles were worth a lot of money. I saw all manner of alcohol befitting of the rich and snobby, not that every rich person is snobby—I think you know what I mean. I saw furniture that was metallic leather sort of. It was soft and supple. I'd love to have one of those chairs. The sofa was to die for, I could tell just by looking at it.

"The pad was vulgar in its luxury. I'm having a hard time explaining this. I'm not saying that it's bad to have fine things. The lighting was amazing. It was embedded in the building materials of the walls and ceiling. They have taken recessed lighting to a level that we've not yet seen. I couldn't tell where the light fixtures were. It seemed like the light was coming from the flat surface itself.

"Sorry to go on about the room like this. I wish I could say something more about life in the future, but I never saw anything beyond the building. So anyway, more about that.

"The colors in the room were predominately black and silver, although a stark purple highlighted the décor. I'm thinking that we should have a sketch artist draw this up so that you can see what's in my mind better. There were many mirrors, but no windows, not a single one.

"I didn't catch a glimpse of the outside world at all, which makes me wonder if there even is an outside world. Maybe these people live in a ruined planet and live entirely in an artificial bubble. I have no idea. It wouldn't surprise me in the slightest. Don't put anything in writing about this though, I saw nothing to indicate what the outside world is like there. I'm just spewing theories.

"Back on track, I don't know how to explain what I mean by a vulgar display of wealth and indulgence. I mean, how is luxury good or bad? How can it feel greedy and hostile? I don't know. I felt this strongly. I suppose that's the best I can do to give you an idea of what the place was like. I picked up on the sense that the little people of their society don't live like that. I bet one square inch of that office could have fed a starving person under their thumb. Again, don't quote me on this. I have nothing more to go on than a gut feeling based on how I felt in that oppressive space.

"Anyway, moving on from that, guess who was sitting at the black marble, or onyx maybe, desk waiting for me? None other than the mysterious Redheaded Devil himself. He did not disappoint. He was as nasty as I thought he'd be if I meet with him in his own territory. He has only one expression, contempt.

"I don't have much to say about meeting with him because we didn't talk long. He got to it quickly, as if he couldn't wait to be rid of me. I felt like vermin. I

121

know he thinks of me that way. He made it clear that I'm scum beneath his feet. I wouldn't be surprised if he had the place sanitized after I left."

Serena stopped for a minute. She stared at her coffee mug that was half empty. She idly realized that she considered it half empty instead of half full. She took a cold sip to refresh her throat. "So, anyway, we made a deal. I'd meet with them and in exchange they'd let our people go. They wanted to send us a message that they can get to us at any time.

"I want to caution us all not to let them defeat us. I'm saying this to myself right now actually. It's intimidating to know that they can snatch us out of our world and into theirs whenever they want to. But they can't destroy us; otherwise they would have already done it. That's something you can quote me on.

"So then they took me to the holding room. Wait, back up, this might be important. I forgot to mention that when I arrived at the Devil's office the other guys didn't come through with me. They must have set my destination for the office and their own for someplace else. I was alone. It was only me and the Red D, warm and cozy. I think we need to remember that they have the ability to pop in and out in multiple directions. Whereas we've yet to try that.

"Technology has obviously improved from what we have today, because I didn't see wristbands on them. They must be doing teleporting and traveling with their minds. I know that this is actually somewhat possible now, and I think we have to start doing it to keep up with them.

"Yes, I'm aware that you have reservations about my ability to control my own thoughts. You think that I'll inadvertently zip off, that I'll get lost in time and space continuum and cause the planet to implode. Dare I say it, you have to trust me. I'm all you've got really.

"You could start over again with another person, but there's only one Serena Wilcox and I'm she. I have something special about me. I really do."

Serena fought to keep the tears from spilling over. She had already lost control once in front of the team. She refused to let that happen again. "I-I happen to know that none of us will be special in the future. There are no more races. There's only the absence of color. There are no genders, but one. There are no babies. There are no children. There are no teenagers. There are no elderly. There are only non-pigmented men in the prime of their lives.

"The humans of the future are not cyborgs. Although parts of them are mechanical, electrical, plastic, animal, and who knows what else, they aren't robots. They're still human.

"From what I understand, they've managed to clone themselves by advancing some of the very technology that we had created for time travel! They've transferred adult memory banks from unknown databases, and they've replicated their adult DNA so that all of them are at the prime of their lives. They are like the Devil said. They are 'us'. That's us in the future unless we change the course of history. And we have to!

"Without a doubt, the future is a hateful world. The absence of color is darkness. The absence of gender is motherless. With no elderly there is no wisdom. With no youth there is no joy. Because their world is perfect, they need no grace. Without grace, there is no love."

Serena looked at her hands and she was stunned by how much they looked like

125

her mother's hands. When had this happened? How long had she had her mother's hands? She was scarcely aware of anyone else in the room. The steady hum of the air purifying system lulled her into a relaxed state. She picked up the coffee mug, now three-quarters empty. She set it back down without drinking any of it.

"I was erased. All women were. I've never felt so invisible in all my life. What value do I have on this Earth? What value do I have to God that He can allow me to be erased? Women were literally extinguished from their world. I say 'their world' because I reject it as my own. This isn't the future of my world. It can't be.

"They say that they have no misogyny because they are one-gendered. They also claim to have no racism. Yes, you guessed it, because they have only one race.

"We were all wrong when describing the MOTF as having white skin. They aren't Caucasian. They have *no pigment at all*. No Caucasian is truly white, there's always a little color mixed in. These people have no color. None!

"Races were destroyed by a depigmentation process. They deliberately inflicted a form of albinism upon themselves. They claim that they did it to eradicate racism, but my take on it is the opposite. Isn't this the most extreme form of racism there can possibly be?

"I'm sorry. I'm having a hard time getting past this. All I know is that I felt a darkness that is hard to define. I never felt so worthless. I was despised and deemed redundant. Worst of all I was disposable. I was insignificant. I had no value. I was not worthy of living.

"Well, my God doesn't say so! I was specially formed in the womb to be born at a specific time. I serve a purpose. I have value. And I'm bound and determined to

127

honor the incredible power that He has entrusted me with. I'm going to change history."

Serena squared her shoulders and for the first time since before she had been taken by the MOTF she looked a bit like her old self. She said, "Einstein told us to do what needs to be done. Who's with me?"

10

Ann Kinji wrapped up the debriefing shortly after Serena finished talking. She told the crew to eat a good meal, get a few winks and consider themselves on call. Then she pushed them out the door.

She immediately contacted the president—in person, without notice. She barged in on a routine press conference, while President Joseph Smythe was still at the podium. The media saw former

President Ann Kinji the moment she stuck her shiny bobbed head into the room. They were all over her.

"Upstaged again." Joe threw his hands up in mock defeat.

Ann shot one meaningful glare at the first photojournalist who dared to shove a camera in her face. The media swarm parted like the Red Sea. She marched up to the podium and planted herself in front of it. Joe brought the microphone down a couple feet. Ann said, "Mr. President has concluded his remarks. I need a moment of his time."

Joe readjusted the microphone back to its previous height. "You'll get a summary of this conference in your media kit." He tipped his pinstriped fedora and followed Ann through the press mob. Joe's short time in office had already brought hats back into fashion, as was evident from how many journalists were also sporting fedoras.

Outside the fray, Joe held the door open for Ann to pass through. "I'm on the road again. We can talk on the way."

Ann marched toward the security detail caravan that lined the exit. Joe's driver opened the door for both her and Joe to climb into the spacious backseat. Ann scurried inside without any effort. Joe crumpled like an accordion to get into the sedan. His fedora clipped the roof of the car as he got in. A member of the security detail caught it before it fell to the pavement, a hat trick that had become a regular show.

With the fedora comfortably back where it belonged on top of the president's head, the privacy barrier between driver and passenger was raised. They were officially alone. "Ann, whatever you need, you've got it."

"I know that, Joe. This isn't a GSI issue. This is an international crisis."

"Can you brief me within fifteen minutes? That's all I've got unless I cancel my stop."

"I can do it in five. The MOTF have committed genocide on a horrific scale. There is no ethnicity, no gender, no young and no old."

"Elaborate."

"They created one gender and one race by eliminating all others through death panels. They are a society of young healthy men, probably between the ages of twenty-one and forty."

There was a long pause as Joe let these words sink in. "The laws of the universe prevent us from intervening."

"We have assurance from Albert Einstein himself that history can be rewritten without catastrophic results."

Joe raised his eyebrows. "Einstein? Your word is enough for me. What do you need?"

Ann leaned in close to Joe to whisper in his ear, in case the sound proofing material was inadequate. "I need the criminally insane."

Joe used a normal speaking volume to respond. "Am I supposed to know what you mean by that?"

Ann's voice was hoarse as she whispered, "The prison still has old technology. Even after what happened in Operation Covert Coffee, the system there was never upgraded."

Joe rubbed his chin with his long fingers. "The MOTF can't spy on you there?"

Ann resumed using her normal speaking voice. "It's worth a try. Beav and Lehman are in agreement that it might work. If they already know our next move, we're done for."

"Of course you can set up shop there. But you didn't need to go to such lengths to get me alone in person. Unless there's something else?"

Ann whispered, "I need Eduardo."

"Now I know why you hijacked my press conference."

"Will you do it?"

The car stopped. "Time's up. I'm headed to my next appointment. The driver can bring you back to GSI."

"Joe, I need to know. Will you do it?"

Joe got out of the vehicle. Before he shut the door he said, "Look for the package to arrive sometime tonight."

11

Serena had a strong feeling that Eduardo knew much more than he'd been telling her. Furthermore, she knew that whatever he said would be unpleasant. To prepare herself for what was sure to be a taxing conversation, she had spent the afternoon in the kitchen.

She made homemade mashed potatoes, roasted chicken, and a wok full of sautéed vegetables. She used her mother's pots and pans. Something about the familiar black-handled pot on the stove settled her. How many dinners had her mother cooked with that same pot? Those were more innocent times, or perhaps more ignorant times. Ignorance is bliss, she told herself.

Serena listened to her children prattle on about their day, talking over each other to get her attention. She fended off Tom's wandering hands as he pestered her while she was at the stove. She laughed, she hugged, and she ate a good meal with her favorite people. Then she picked up the green scarf that Jo had given her at the beginning of her work on Project Scarecrow.

The world was counting on Serena to be the person that she was born to be. She could do this, she really could. Telling herself that she couldn't was unacceptable, and not even true. No, there was no way out, only a way through.

It was this mindset that she carried into her meeting with Eduardo. She greeted him quickly, lest her expression reveal her shock at how haggard he looked. He was even worse off than when she'd last seen him. His hiding place apparently didn't include a razor, and from the smell of him he hadn't had a shower in a good while.

Before they could begin they were interrupted by a prison guard. "Ms. Wilcox, you have a visitor."

Serena gasped. Standing two feet in front of her was a deranged looking woman with wild hair and a sloppy smile. She recognized her as Lita, an inmate there at the prison for the criminally insane. Serena had helped put Lita in this facility. "Hello Lita. I see that you're the same as always. What do you want?"

Lita tossed her mane with great vigor. "No, no. It's about what *you* want."

Serena sighed. "What is it that you think I want, Lita."

Lita cackled. "Not so fast. I want something too."

"Naturally. I'd expect nothing less."

"I want you to get me out on good behavior."

Serena groaned. "Have you had good behavior, Lita?"

Lita gave Serena a loopy smile and blinked her eyes rapidly. "Absolutely not."

"Lita, they aren't going to let you out. You threatened the life of a United States president, among other things. I can't help you. Do the right thing and talk to me anyway."

Lita chewed her lower lip for a few seconds. Then her eyes widened, showing alarmingly dilated pupils. "I want something else then."

"I'm listening."

"I want the satisfaction of knowing that I've done the right thing." Lita blew bubbles out through her nose, thrashed around like she was being Tasered, and then spun around in circles until she fell down.

Serena watched her flop around like a fish on the beige-painted cement floor. "Get up, Lita."

Lita popped back up and pretended to dust herself off. Then, sounding completely rational as if she hadn't just put on a freak show, she launched into her spiel. "Are you listening? I have been. We can still see what goes on in the crack between the Social Media Channel. No one ever did seal that up and we've been watching conversations going on in there. Usually it's a hangout for perverts and they are dull to listen to. Every Wednesday the real entertainment comes in. We watch

139

them talk to each other when they think that no one can see them. Nobody cares about us in here. We don't count."

Serena clapped her hands. "Ahah! I thought so! The old system is still clunky and obsolete – and a good place to hide. But of course we aren't the only ones to have thought of it. Who's using it? Tell me as much as you can."

Lita pouted. "See? You don't count us as people. Nobody's hiding from *us*. *We* can see them. No one cares if we see them. We're nothing but animals to the outside world."

"I see you. I'm listening."

Lita considered this for a few seconds. "I'll tell you what you want to know, even though you've done nothing to deserve it. I'm the only one around here who ever does anything and yet people want more and more of me."

Serena waited for Lita to continue as minutes dripped through the hourglass. Finally Lita said, "Here's the deal. Every Wednesday, like I said, we tune in. The regular characters on any other given day are losers and cretins. But on Wednesday, glorious Wednesday, we finally get to watch something interesting. That's when the Supporters come on."

Serena's facial expression gave her away.

Lita sniggered. "I know something the great and powerful Serena Wilcox doesn't. What's the matter, have they fallen out of love with you?"

Eduardo spoke up. "Ladies, you'll have to speed this along. If you want something from me you're going to run out of time to get it."

Serena wasn't sure which way to turn her attention. She decided not to choose one over another, but to alternate

141

questions between the two. Her experiment annoyed Eduardo but Lita was in her element. Serena began with Eduardo. "I want to know how the depigmentation program began."

Eduardo's eyes shifted from left to right. He tugged on his mustache and then opened his mouth to speak. Serena held up her index finger. "Hold that thought. Lita, yes, it threw me that the Supporters are utilizing the old Social Media Channel. Have they asked for me?"

Lita nodded her head like a wooden puppet. "Yes. They asked for you."

"What? Why didn't you contact me? When did they ask for me? Wait, hold that thought. Eduardo, about the depigmentation program, where do I find the people working on that project?" He didn't respond. "Oh come on, I know you must be working on the early stages of it now, in present day."

Eduardo pulled on his mustache while speaking. "Melanocytes are the cells responsible for skin pigmentation. When those cells die or stop functioning, it causes a condition known as vitiligo in which the skin loses color and becomes patchy. Depigmentation agents are commonly used to create a uniform look to the skin. The skin then becomes quite pale. Those agents also unfortunately create a problem; they create intolerance to sun exposure. We're working on alternative ways to produce depigmentation of the skin. Vitiligo used to affect only one percent of the world's population but due to the rise of immune system disorders and unknown causes, vitiligo now affects over thirty-one percent of the world's population and we expect that number to rise, especially among dark skinned people."

"OK, I don't think I need to know any of that. I want to know who's working on it. How do I find them?" Serena looked at Lita. "And you—answer me, when did the Supporters ask for me and why wasn't I contacted?"

Lita was smug. "They asked for you just now. They said that they knew you'd be in today because you told them. You *did* time travel! I knew it. You look like you're from the future."

"What? Never mind, that's not important. I'll jump onto the system to talk to them as soon as I'm done with Eduardo here. So, then, Eduardo, who's 'we'? Who's working on the project, besides you apparently?"

Eduardo spoke quickly. "I have nothing to do with it. I only meant scientists in general, researchers. I wasn't any part of the depigmentation program, but I can confirm that it does indeed exist

144

and that they are getting close to making a key discovery the last that I heard. That was over a year ago. They may have broken through by now. As for how to find them, that's easy."

Serena turned her attention back toward Lita. "You don't have anything more to add. Am I right?"

Lita's non-answer was confirmation enough. Serena signaled to the guard that she was ready for Lita to be escorted back to her cell.

"That leaves you and me, Eduardo. The team is waiting in the common room and they can help me obtain the rest of what I need from you."

"Which is?"

"I want you to give me more data so that I can go further back in time."

Eduardo picked at his mustache. "I've given you enough of a time window for anything you could possibly need."

145

Serena looked away from his mustache picking. "I need to go someplace where the MOTF can't find me. They don't have the data to go back farther than our archives and their current technology is based on those archives. I chose this facility to talk to you because they can't hack into it. But they'll figure it out. If I go back in time further than they can travel I can speak openly with my team, at least until they catch on to what I'm doing. Is it 'further' or 'farther'?"

Eduardo gritted his teeth.

Serena continued. "The entire prison is off the grid. The government hasn't gotten around to committing dollars and time to updating it. There are few other areas in this country that don't have towers, wireless ears, and other ways of bugging or tapping. We're encased in concrete here, and underground if you haven't noticed. We're as safe as we can be, without traveling farther back in time to where they can't travel. So, anyway, I brought you here so that you can give me the data without them knowing, hopefully, like I said. And after you do that for me, I'm going to secretly travel back to a time period that the MOTF can't follow me to."

"I understand what you want. The problem is that I don't have any data to give you. If we use our current time window to retrieve the data, the MOTF will see us. Perhaps you haven't thought this through."

Serena swept her long hair into a ponytail and wrapped an elastic band around it. "Let's not panic. I'm confident that the future me has this covered. I need to sign on to the Social Media Channel. I'm guessing the Supporters are waiting."

Eduardo sniffed. "You didn't know about this development with the

Supporters until you got here. What was your plan before that?"

Serena turned on the Social Media Channel and squinted at the screen. It was hard to adjust to the old technology. Fortunately someone was waiting for her. "It's about time you showed up!" His voice sounded familiar.

Serena shrugged. "I did the best I could. I only got the message a few minutes ago. Can you help me get time travel data or does my question mean nothing to you?"

"I know exactly what this is about. You wanted us to upload the data here. All you have to do is retrieve it. This is Bob, by the way. You might remember me."

"Yes, I remember you. How did you get the data?"

Bob chuckled. "You'll find out in three, two…"

The guard rapped at the door. Serena and Eduardo froze, their minds racing to guess who might be on the other side of it. Serena said, "Yes?"

The door opened and in walked Malirah and James Edison, the two scientists from Project Scarecrow who had moved on. Malirah smiled. "Now you know what we were working on. *You* are the one, the future Serena anyway, who recruited us away from GSI! And Eduardo here too, he's been in on it also. Even though the government has been fooled into believing that he was sequestered for the purpose of witness relocation, the real reason for hiding him was to hide him from you! It's been painfully rough to keep this a secret from you, but you insisted that you couldn't know about this until exactly the right moment. You came close to figuring it out and outsmarting yourself."

Serena's jaw dropped. "I can't believe that I didn't see this coming. But now that I know, you can come back to GSI, right? Why did I want you to hide in the first place?"

Malirah said, "You had requested that we create a second investigation team, one that was kept secret even from you. Its purpose was to evade the prying eyes of the MOTF. You divided the tasks amongst the GSI team and our covert one, with everyone's input of course. And so far, it's worked. I'd call this a success. But it's far from over. We'll have to go back into our faux witness relocation program. It's too early for us to emerge."

"How will I contact you? What if I want your help with something in the here and now?"

Bob interjected, "Hey, Serena, you can hash these things out later. I've been waiting around for you for most of the day. The files are ready to download. If you run into any problems, you can reach me by my old contact number."

Serena waved him off. "Thanks Bob. It was good to see you." His connection logged off. "I assume those files are important."

Malirah reached out and grabbed her arm. "Let Eduardo take care of that. We need to talk. Have a seat."

Serena winced. "I have to sit down? This can't be good."

James Edition cleared his throat. "We've been working on finding a way to retrieve data to go further back into the past, so that you can go somewhere where the MOTF can't find you."

Serena glared at Eduardo. "You knew what I wanted all along? Was all of that really necessary? You were a tad condescending."

151

James said, "He was convincing. Serena, focus on what I'm telling you. You were right, you can work in the past out of their reach. They can't spy on you there, as long as you keep things moving. It's a brilliant plan. But it has problems, or should I say *had* problems. We've already done this. You might say I'm the future James."

Serena looked from James to Malirah to Eduardo. "I don't much like it that I'm from the past when all of you are from the future."

Malirah patted her on the head. "Your ego can take it. Listen up. Finding a way to get the data without the MOTF seeing us was an obstacle, but we've done it!"

"How? How did you do it?"

Malirah said, "We sent Eduardo back to Davenport, Iowa, 1939, to the orphanage. He was already there retrieving data for the MOTF, remember? It was easy for him to slip back again without raising suspicion. And, unbeknownst to the MOTF, he retrieved data not only from the orphans, but also from the oldest person he could find. He recruited someone he saw walking past the orphanage picture window, an elderly woman out for a walk. Eduardo sent a child from the orphanage outside, to ask the woman to please come in. She did, and best of all, she agreed to an experiment that could 'help the children'. Because Eduardo never left the building, no one saw anything. We are certain that the MOTF don't know anything about this. He retrieved the data from this kind soul, which has opened our time window considerably. You can now journey further into the past, and you'll be safe from the prying eyes of the MOTF. The mission was far easier than we expected it to be."

Serena leapt to her feet. "Wonderful!"

Malirah scolded her. "Not so fast." She held out her arm and gently pushed Serena back into the chair.

James Edison said, "There's more. You also wanted us to perfect the mind-driven time travel method. You wanted to have the same control over time travel, or teleportation as some of us are calling it now, that the MOTF do. And that's commendable. I was on your side."

Malirah added, "It's a shame though. You were so fond of Ruby Red. But, you want to take them off guard at some point, that's what you said. Let me bring it to your attention that you can only play that card once. After they know you can time travel freely, you won't have the element of surprise to use again. Choose that moment wisely."

Serena said, "Why am I sitting for this? I understand that I can only take them by surprise once. Is there more? Don't leave me hanging in suspense."

Malirah and James Edison exchanged a dramatic look. "There could be complications," said James.

"What kind of 'complications'?"

Malirah's voice lost a little of its typical boom. "There's a possibility that you'll suck people into your time travel portal, meaning yourself, since you are the portal. If people stand too close to you when you are materializing, it could be bad. It hasn't been thoroughly tested. I have to warn you, we had an incident."

"You may as well tell me."

James Edison explained, "I was channeling my thoughts to travel back to present day when I was standing near another person. That person turned up with me, except, uh, not completely."

Serena blanched. "What does that mean, 'not completely'?"

155

James Edison choked up and left the room. Malirah had to finish. "He means that the other person didn't fully materialize on the other side. She, well, she died. It was rather gruesome actually."

Serena gasped.

Eduardo, who had been silent this entire time, said, "We did go back to resolve the issue. We were able to reverse the damage. Rest assured, that woman is alive and well in the time period in which she belongs."

Malirah was quick to add, "But unfortunately James Edison will never be the same, nor will we. It was truly a horrific sight. I don't want to witness anything of that nature ever again."

Serena said, "If it does, could we reverse it as you did before?"

Malirah pondered this. "I don't know. I can't guarantee it. But partner travel does work successfully when following one

156

simple rule. If you want to bring someone with you, make sure that the two of you are physically touching. Any physical contact will do, even if you are only touching their clothes or purse strap. Anything connected to their body will work, and vice versa. Do not let go during materialization."

Eduardo said, "Before we run out of time there are a couple of issues that you had brought up back at GSI. Lehman supplied me with the transcripts of all of your briefings and I've been chewing on those. Don't look so surprised—did you think that I wouldn't micromanage my own program? Time travel is my life's work, remember that."

Serena said, "I haven't forgotten."

Eduardo continued, "First, that question you had about the WWI soldiers mentioning Hitler, who didn't rise to power until WWII, is of valid concern. The time window develops a weak point when too many travelers interact with the natural order of time and space. Consider it like bending plastic back and forth, back and forth until it breaks. That's an imperfect example, but it will suffice. You didn't break through the time window—no serious harm was done. However, you did get a warning of what could happen if you do this. Avoid large numbers of travelers in the same time window at the same time, especially if the MOTF will also be there in the same space. The combination of too many people and too many people traveling from different fixed points is the cocktail you don't want to drink."

Serena blinked. "Did you just make a clever analogy, Eduardo? I had no idea that you were so witty."

Eduardo smoothed out his tired mustache. "There's something else. Your time window is based on data we extracted from the memories of human beings, and as you know, human memories are unreliable. The WWI soldiers' mention of Hitler may have been a result of someone's mind slipping. In other words, it may have been a result of faulty data and therefore my warning about too many travelers in the time window is invalid in this scenario, but still valid as an overall concern regardless. Do you follow what I'm staying? You'll make an alternate history. That's not good, Serena, in case you didn't make that assumption."

Serena stood up. "I'll try not to screw up."

"Fair enough." Eduardo sighed.

"One more thing, what happens if someone's mind is way out of whack? Will I end up in the ice age being chased by a giant lizard?" Serena grinned.

Eduardo's face reddened. "The ice age? You're... yes, I see you're yanking my

159

chain. Ha, ha. Well, let's stay on track for the thirty or so seconds we have remaining. Let me assure you that we don't extract samples from deranged or delusional individuals! Faulty data is rare and inconsequential. Adolf Hitler didn't show up in the Argonne Forest of World War 1, did he? Of course not! He was mentioned in a conversation, in an almost trivial exchange. While it is unpleasant to discover imperfect data, it is important to note that this isolated event, this anomaly, didn't damage the time window. That's a fine example of what I'm talking about. You'll experience a few inconsistencies but I don't anticipate that these glitches will result in any significant events."

Serena said, "Got it. Let's get back to that other thing. What if someone gets accidentally sucked in when I'm time traveling. How do I avoid that?"

Eduardo said, "People accompanying you should be tethered to you physically, we've covered this already. Passerby must be at least three feet away from you before teleportation or traveling, lest they be at risk for an unintended consequence."

Serena said, "And if they aren't? They will die?"

Eduardo nodded. "The odds of that are ninety-nine percent."

"Out of a hundred?"

"Of course out of..." Eduardo stopped short when he saw the smirk on Serena's face. "I must say, I find your humor to be ill timed and grossly inappropriate."

Serena shrugged, as she was fond of doing. "So I've been told." She noticed that Eduardo was desperately pulling on his now-sparse mustache. "I recommend that you get a sense of humor and some mustache wax."

161

12

Serena was out of her depth when talking to the team of scientists responsible for the depigmentation research project, but she bulldozed through her academic shortcomings. "Nothing is supposed to travel faster than the speed of light, therefore going back in time should be impossible but we've proven otherwise."

Serena paused to skim over her notes. "Einstein believed in a cosmological principle, of a uniform and unchanging universe that was actually at odds with his theory of general relativity. Einstein came up with the concept of 'repulsive gravity' to explain how the universe could be static, and yet not static I suppose. I don't know if these are as related as I'm making them out to be, but I want to talk now about 'causality'. Causality requires that cause and effect are so important that their order can't be reversed. You can't be born before your mother."

She continued, "Einstein said, about his theory of relativity, that mass and energy are different manifestations of the same thing, 'a somewhat unfamiliar concept for the average man'. And in his famous equation, $E=mc^2$, he illustrates that mass and energy are equivalent. In other words, or should I say, in my words, Einstein asserts that the two seemingly different things may actually be two sides of the same coin."

Serena couldn't get a pulse on what these scientists were thinking. She hurried through the rest of her speech. "I'm saying all of this to convince you that what I'm asking you to do won't cause a paradox or implosion or something. Whatever God…"

She noticed that the mention of God caused a few of the scientists to flinch. The last thing she wanted was to create division and distraction. Serena moved on.

"Whatever is intended for the human race, we can't alter it. The universe is static. While it appears to be flexible and changing, the overall picture remains unchanged and has already been written. We shouldn't fear that anything we do, or don't do, can throw the universe off of its track. We aren't that powerful.

I think of it this way: do you ever look at paintings that have all the little dots? What's that called?" No one offered an answer.

She struggled to come up with it and then said triumphantly, "Pointillism! Yes, that's what I was going for. It's a form of art in which the painter has created the whole picture with many tiny dots of paint. If you look at it up close it's all nonsense, nothing but a lot of random dots. But from a distance, the dots form a complete and beautiful picture. If I were to rearrange a few of those tiny dots, or even remove a few altogether, it wouldn't have any effect on the painting as a whole. From a distance, the painting would look unchanged. This is how it all makes sense to me. I feel confident in asking you to alter the course of history. Thank you for your patience as I've worked up to my reason for being here."

Serena paused. No one seemed the least bit curious about what she was doing here, even though it was clear that nobody knew what was going on. Her confidence faltered some but she finished her presentation. "The research you are doing will cause more harm than good. That's why I'm here today to beg you to stop your research on depigmentation."

An olive-skinned woman in a bold orange pantsuit with large cornered lapels stood up and strode to Serena's side. She said, "You must tell us more if you expect us to abandon even one hour of our life's work."

A murmur rose from the rest of the team. Serena held up her hands. "I know, I know. How dare I do this, right? I'm sorry. I really am. But you have to stop. I wish I could explain more."

The orange-suited woman returned to her seat, but not before saying, "You must tell us specifically what damage our research has done in the future if you expect us to abandon it in the present."

Serena's eyebrows furrowed. "That's only fair, I know. Persuasion requires understanding, and if I'm to persuade you to willingly abandon your depigmentation project, you need to know why I'm asking you to do it. However, in the absence of understanding, I'll resort to coercion to get you to do what I want."

The scientists stirred. Serena continued, "I see that you're finally interested in what I'm saying. I have authority from the President himself to force you to cease and desist. I came to you with a direct appeal to persuade you. I don't believe that you need coercion, as your desire for this research is to heal, not harm. I regret that we can't fully disclose everything that we know, but I can do my best to…"

A young scientist who couldn't have been much over twenty years old said, "Are you saying that you're shutting us down?"

"We have the authority to force you to comply, but I trust that you'll want to do the right thing. Please hear me out, now that you're finally listening to me. What if I told you how your research will be abused in the future? Everyone will be 'depigmented' until there is only one race. You can see the evil in this, right?"

No one said anything as they digested the news. The woman in the orange suit broke the uneasy quiet. "You can verify this?"

"Yes."

"May we see this verification?" the woman asked.

"This is highly classified information, which is why we had to put you through security checks and make you sign a gag

169

order. I brought along a recording from an official GSI briefing on this manner. That's the best I can do. The less you know, the better, trust me on this."

The woman in the orange suit, the apparent spokesperson for the group, finally introduced herself. "I am Maude. I believe in what you say. But there is no need to fully abandon our research if you tell me which project has created this outcome. We will divert resources away from that prong and concentrate on other avenues."

"I'm concerned that any research toward depigmentation will result in the same outcome. I'm afraid that I can't take no for an answer."

Maude shook her head. "We will not shut down until we know more specifically. We must have more details, more scientific details."

Eduardo emerged at that moment. The unfortunate trailing of toilet paper on the bottom of his shoe gave them all a clue as to where he had been. He was startled by the immediate attention on him. Serena patted him on the arm. "You can take it from here, right?"

Before Eduardo could respond, Serena walked briskly out into the dark corridor toward freedom. She walked even faster when she heard the scientist's voices erupt from the room as soon as the door was closed. Serena imagined Eduardo tugging fervently at his mustache. He's going to pull that thing right off his face one of these days, she thought.

Natalie Buske Thomas

13

Mandolin wasn't officially involved in anything at the moment. He wasn't offended. He knew that he wasn't the man to go to when someone needed a thinker.

But they were underestimating him all the same. Mandolin knew how the MOTF operated. Whether from the past, present or future, men like them were all the same. Too cocky for their own good, their arrogance kept them from believing that anyone would be able to catch them.

Mandolin found the MOTF spying on them no more than a few blocks from the GSI building. Without their gadgets these men were inferior fighters. Besides, Mandolin had the home team advantage. He didn't hesitate in his approach.

Mandolin saw the driver in the first black sedan. It was the same experience as it was when he had first met the Redheaded Devil. He was hiding under the brim of his hat, behind his shades, and under poorly applied synthetic facial hair. Mandolin couldn't believe it was actually him. Then again, he wasn't sure that it was.

Mandolin had originally described the Redheaded Devil as Caucasian. It was only later that he learned that the Devil had no race at all, and was instead depigmented, not that he understood what that meant. But this man didn't look unearthly pale. He

174

looked like a regular white guy. Mandolin wondered if maybe he thought all white men looked the same. No, he told himself, he knew what he was seeing. This was not a depigmented face. This was definitely a common variety white guy, he was sure of it. Was this not the Redheaded Devil?

The driver removed his shades and rubbed his eyes. He glanced up and saw Mandolin staring at him. The two men locked eyes. A flicker of recognition washed over both of their faces.

The Devil moved fast, but Mandolin moved faster. Why did people always leave their windows open for him? Mandolin reached into the sedan and repeated what he had done the last time he had encountered this vile man. He grabbed his faux beard and ripped it off of his face. Except this time around, he didn't toss the artificial hair into the backseat. He jammed it into his pants pocket. He had a hunch that Ms. Wilcox would want to see it.

The driver laughed. "What does that prove? You already know who I am."

Mandolin grabbed him by the shirt collar, knocking the Devil's hat off in the process. His red hair sprang out like a snake from a can. Mandolin forced the Devil out of the car. It was light work for a man of Mandolin's size.

The Devil sniggered. "What do you think you've accomplished? I'll teleport when I tire of you."

Mandolin hadn't factored in the Devil's one and only super power, but he didn't let this intimidate him. Mandolin popped the Devil square in the face with his heavy hand. He was so consumed with his own cleverness, the Devil never saw it coming.

14

Serena blinked. "Is that who I think it is?"

Mandolin huffed and groaned as he lumbered into the briefing room with the Devil slung over his shoulder. He dropped the body onto the table with a soft thud.

"Is he dead?" asked Beav.

Mandolin's forehead tightened. "What do you take me for? No, he's not dead.

And I got you this too." He tossed the artificial hair onto the Devil's chest.

"So, he's just knocked out then," Serena clarified.

Mandolin grunted.

Serena stared at the Redheaded Devil lying on the table. "He's white! I mean, he's a *shade* of white. There's pigment in his skin, he's Caucasian! He's not... what are we calling it? Race-less? Eduardo must have struck a deal with the scientists—no more research into depigmentation! We did it! We did it! It's a victory for all of humankind! It's a victory for ..."

Beav tapped Serena's shoulder. "As soon as he comes to he'll teleport out of here. What's your plan?"

Serena pointed at Lehman.

Lehman looked around the room. "Who me? What do you want me to do?"

"Hook us up with an anesthesiologist."

Lehman asked, "You're sedating him?"

Beav said, "If he's awake, he'll never stay."

Serena agreed. "Right. We should sedate him, like Lehman said."

Lehman protested, "I didn't recommend that. I was saying what I thought *you* were saying."

Serena said, "When he's out cold we'll pull DNA samples of everything. His fingernails, his hair, his skin, everything!"

"Too late, he's coming around." Beav rushed to the table, but the Devil saw Beav coming toward him. He vaporized from his prone position on his table before anyone could stop him. When his body vanished the artificial hair that had been resting on the Devil's chest fell to the tabletop.

Serena grabbed it. "We've got this. Let's at least run DNA on this." She tossed the beard at Lehman who caught it with one hand.

Beav said, "You guys shouldn't be playing catch with it. You aren't even wearing gloves." He snapped a glove on his right hand and said, "Give me that, I'll take it down to the lab."

Estep said, "You've tried this already. You said that his DNA was scrambled so we can't ID him."

Beav said, "That's right, I said 'scrambled', but not gone. All the data we need is still there. If we get enough samples for comparison we'll eventually have enough material to decipher his true DNA. I don't know how many samples it will take. We might be able to crack the code now, with only this one additional sample. Then again, it could take hundreds more samples. We're dealing with unfamiliar technology."

Serena said, "We won't stop until we find out who he is. He came from somewhere. He's related to someone." She shivered. "Maybe when he told me that he's me in the future, he wasn't speaking in generalities. Maybe he meant that he's related to me somehow. Maybe he meant that he *is* me in the future."

Estep bellowed, "Oh he is not! Knock that off!"

Serena said, "Well, he's related to somebody. Let's find his ancestors alive today."

"And then what? Sterilize them?" asked Estep.

Beav said, "That's a good question. Do you have a plan?"

Serena felt all eyes on her. Lehman, Estep, Beav and Mandolin waited for her to answer. "I'm working on it."

Mandolin cleared his throat, "I'll be off unless you need me."

Serena said, "Good work today. I'll need you again, so don't go too far. Although, the Devil doesn't seem to be particularly strong. I bet I could take him."

"Oh for crying... You can't either!" Estep was working himself up into a frenzy until he caught Serena winking at him. "Oh, I see, you were joking. Wait until you're the damsel in distress and I have to bail you out."

Serena smiled broadly. "I seem to recall that it was me who bailed you out."

Mandolin slipped out the door. His next stop was Ann Kinji's office. He knew that Serena couldn't handle herself against the MOTF. Since she had all but invited him along on their mission, it was time to talk to Ann about getting one of those bracelets. He would let Serena go on ahead and then secretly shadow her. His method had worked well the first time he had time travelled and he was confident that his method would work for as long as he needed to use it.

Mandolin's idea was an easy sell to Ann, but she instructed him to sit this one out. "You don't look like an immigrant and there's not enough time to pull something together for you. But I do want you equipped to go with them on the next mission. I agree, it's a good idea to have you along when the Extreme Team isn't deployed."

"Where are they headed right now?" he asked.

"The opening day celebration of Ellis Island, January 1, 1892."

15

The first federal immigrant inspection station on Ellis Island was three-stories tall and opened with a celebration on January 1, 1892. Seven hundred immigrants from three separate ships passed over the docks on that first day. About five years later, on June 15, 1897, a fire of unknown origin turned the wooden structures on Ellis Island into ashes. This event was of utmost importance to Serena because most of the immigration records were destroyed.

Serena didn't say much to the crew before their mission. The whole point of the operation was to speak without the MOTF listening in. She waited until just before the launch before giving them the letter she had prepared. She instructed them to read it now.

"I chose Ellis Island opening day, because three large ships came in with hundreds of immigrants—almost a thousand, all arriving on the same day. We'll blend in easily with all that chaos. Anyone who doesn't recognize us as fellow passengers from their own ship will assume that we came from one of the other two ships. Thanks to Beav's production team our papers are authentic enough to pass an inspection, but I hope to not ever make it to the window. If we do get processed, don't worry. We won't alter history with a permanent record of our arrival on Ellis Island. The records burned in 1897. All trace of us having been there will be gone then. But it's best if we finish our meeting before we make it through the inspection line. Please exit now under one of the two tents, men on the right and women on the left. You'll find your wardrobe kit. Dress quickly and be ready to teleport."

The crew finished reading their letters and headed into the tents that had been erected just before dawn, while still under cover of darkness. They dressed as quickly as they could, but it was challenging to handle all of the fasteners and extra layers. When they were ready, they marveled at how dapper they all looked in their period piece clothing.

Jo, Malirah and Serena wore dresses with a tight bodice, a skirt gathered at the waist, leg o'mutton sleeves, and an almost

187

bell-like silhouette. Each also wore a hat adorned with ribbon. They wore coats, but the design left much room for chill. They fortunately also carried a travel blanket that they could wrap around them in a pinch.

The women left their tent for 1892 without returning to the tarmac, as they didn't want the MOTF to catch a glimpse of them on one of the many cameras focused on the tarmac. Beav, Estep and Lehman followed the same protocol, so it was only after arriving on Ellis Island that they all saw each other.

The men wore a gray or navy overcoat coat with a matching waistcoat, dark trousers and a floppy bow tie. Beav was unwilling to cut his hair for this exercise so he had pinned it tightly against his scalp to give the appearance of having short hair. Lehman and Estep wore faux pointed beards. Beav needed only to groom and gel his goatee.

The six of them had materialized at 1892 Ellis Island during the precise moment when one of the ships had docked. Eduardo had programmed their arrival to place them on the north side of one of the outbuildings, an area that offered no clear view of the docks and was therefore likely to be vacant. Eduardo's hunch was correct. They were alone when they arrived at Ellis Island. However, they would arouse suspicion eventually if they loitered there. They walked at a brisk pace until they successfully merged with the crowd.

Seeing the immigrants was more emotional than Serena had anticipated it would be. Their eyelids were heavy, their cheeks were drawn and sunken, and their clothes draped over their bodies, revealing that they had lost weight during their long voyage. Some were noticeably ill.

189

She saw mainly first and second class
passengers milling around, as they were
allowed to exit the ship before the steerage
class. If Serena and crew had worn
working class clothing, they would have
been assumed to be steerage class
passengers, who must exit last. They risked
arriving ahead of them. To avoid this
pitfall, Eduardo had suggested a wardrobe
befitting of the social elite so that they
would fit in well with the first arrivals.

Only the first and second class
passengers were immediately allowed to
dock. Ordinarily the steerage-class would
have been ferried to Ellis Island for
inspection, where they were subjected to
physical examinations and marked with
chalk to indicate if they were ill. But today
it was a mash of the upper and lower
classes, due to the opening day celebration,
and because new regulations hadn't come

about until the immigration laws of the 1920's.

It was after the steerage class disembarked that Serena choked up. She could tell just by looking at these people that they probably hadn't seen daylight in weeks. They wore the stench of the ship on their bodies—it was a smell that was palpable. Someone barked orders for men to go one way, women and children a different direction. One father told his children to meet back at the pile of luggage and hope that they could find one another again. Several children appeared to be traveling alone.

Despite the obvious signs of human suffering, Serena was overwhelmed by a pining that glimmered in their weary eyes. These people believed in America, in this land that had yet to experience the terrorism of September 11, 2001, the great market crash, or the Big War. For them this was the land of the free, a safe haven. And so it would be, for many years to come.

Beav shook Serena out of her reverie. "We should get on with this."

Serena gestured for everyone to gather close together. She wasn't concerned about passerby overhearing her because the immigration inspection station was the perfect cover, given the wide variety of languages and accents all around them. However, the din made it hard for the crew to hear Serena's soft voice.

"We need to get out of here as soon as we can. So, let's get to it. First, the good news. It looks like we succeeded in preventing the depigmentation program from morphing out into ethnic cleansing. The bad news? We've only just begun this fight. My children will likely still be alive when some of these evildoings will come to pass, and my grandchildren most definitely. I'm doing this for them. This is about my kids, and everyone's. We have to stop the MOTF. But we can't keep meeting in places like this." More immigrants had pooled into the inspection area. With hundreds of bodies engulfing them, the smell coming off of the unwashed and ill travelers was packing a punch that brought Jo to the gagging point. She coughed into her hand.

Estep said, "What alternatives do we have? Passing notes in invisible ink? Dead drops, old school Russian spy tricks?"

Serena said, "I was hoping that one of you would say that we can make a bug-free environment, if only one office. Our tent idea worked to give us temporary cover on the tarmac. Can't we come up with a permanent solution?"

Beav said, "We can't use encryption and we can't outpace them in technology, so we're limited."

193

Serena said, "But it's not an impossible idea?"

Lehman said, "What he's getting at is that we can't use computers. Unless you want to go back to the prison and set up there, nothing digitally transmitted is safe."

Serena said, "At this point I just want to be able to communicate with you in plain sight right there at GSI so that we don't have to resort to this way of meeting. Lehman can still record our briefings. We don't need to back them up digitally."

Beav said, "If that's all you want then, yes, we can do it. I have a few ideas for constructing a room within a room, but I'm afraid we'll be in a storage closet. I can't figure out how to find their bugs. I'm working on the assumption that they didn't bother with closets."

Jo said, "That sounds like a reasonable assumption, but why not team up with Lehman and a few others to give it another try? We'd be better off if we knew how they are spying on us."

Malirah said, "Remember, Serena, you were using Eduardo, James and me as a secondary investigative team. I don't know why you let that fizzle. We were doing good work. We can go back in time before GSI was bugged, examine it with a fine toothed comb, go back to present day and do a comparison. We could find the anomalies and eliminate the surveillance."

Serena said, "Removing the bugs would tip our hand. They need to think that they are spying on us as usual. I want a safe room that they don't know about. I think the storage closet idea could work, but they'll see us coming and going into it. It won't take long before they bug the closet too."

Beav said, "I'll have to set up an optical illusion. I'm going to need mirrors, a sound system and some robotics. It'll be a challenge." He suddenly lowered his voice. "We're attracting attention from that official looking gentleman on my right."

Serena hurried. "But you can do it?"

Beav said, "I can do it."

Serena looked back at the gentleman that Beav had brought to her attention. He was walking purposely toward them. She said, "Now would be a good time to go."

The crew followed Serena into the heart of the smelly and exhausted immigrants, with their many tattered blankets, parcels and bags. From there, they disappeared one by one from Ellis Island 1892 back to present day GSI. They reappeared in the tents, changed their clothes, exited the tents, and packed everything up before the sun gave them away.

16

Beav flew down the GSI corridor, slipping and sliding in his boldly striped felted "toe-sock" shoes. The gossip mill reported that GSI was considering imposing a dress code to curtail Beav from expressing himself. For now he was free to wear what he wanted to work, but the toe-socks were his own undoing. Beav skidded around the corner and promptly did a face-plant.

Agent Estep had serendipitously also been en route to Ann's office at that very moment. He was finishing the last bite of his sandwich when he witnessed Beav taking a dive. "Dinner *and* a show!"

Beav bounced back onto his feet and dusted off his clothes. "Show's over. You saw nothing."

Estep laughed until he choked on his sandwich.

Serena joined them. "What are you two nits doing?"

Before they could answer, Ann Kinji opened her office door. "I can give you ten minutes."

Serena said, "Perhaps a time when you're not busy would be better." She extended her hand toward Ann.

Ann shook it. The handshake was their signal to meet in the safe room. Serena, Beav and Estep went ahead to the now high-tech storage closet while Ann

198

feigned a few minutes of work at her desk before leaving her office. She found most of the crew waiting for her in the cramped space of the storage closet. "What's this about?"

Beav took a deep breath. His eyes were wild. "They've done it. The lab found enough DNA in the artificial hair to descramble the block. We have it. We have the Red Devil's DNA."

Ann smiled. "Good work. Give me an update when you know more. I have a meeting with GSI investors and I was hoping to grab something to eat first." She eyed Estep's chin. "I see you must have already had your lunch."

Estep had a trail of peanut butter running from the corner of the right side of his mouth down to his chin. The former president of the United States catching Estep with peanut butter drool, versus Beav's face-plant in the hall—it was a tough call. Beav clapped Estep on the shoulder. "We're even," he said.

"What do we do now?" asked Serena.

"We wait. We have the DNA, but we don't have an ancestry match yet. Stick around though. I expect more information within the hour," said Beav.

The crew dispersed. Only Lehman hung back to switch out the tapes for their next briefing. Using old school technology was a bear, but better safe than sorry.

While the rest of the crew gathered in the break room Serena wandered outside onto the tarmac. She looked wistfully at Ruby Red. It wasn't that long ago, less than a year, since she had first laid eyes on the glorious metallic egg-shaped portal. Serena felt like she had aged a decade since then. She peeked inside. The flowers had died.

Had she really expected that someone would have attended to the planter, even though Ruby Red had been all but abandoned? If the flowers had been important to her she should have watered them herself. Besides, there wasn't enough air or light in the portal. Without regularly removing the planter the flowers would have died anyway.

She squinted her eyes against the glare of GSI's glass exterior. She couldn't see inside the building but since no one was yet coming out, she gave herself permission to relax for a few minutes.

Serena climbed into the Ruby Red portal, closed the hatch, and settled into the seat. She nearly squashed the neglected pilot's hat that she'd left there. The hat had been ceremoniously gifted to her by Malirah and Jo before her first mission. She stroked the leather material before putting it on her head.

She leaned back into the headrest and reflected upon her career thus far. Her early days as a private detective had involved sporadic contract work. To mask her desperation for steady employment, she had often been silly and flippant. This had worked well to get her through social tension in the short term, but her lack of professionalism had failed to impress.

She hadn't been mature enough to understand that she wasn't comfortable in her own skin. She had bounced around too much, she hadn't been able to stay focused, she hadn't been consistent, she had meandered, she had had some good ideas but hadn't executed them well, and she had been inappropriately humorous during serious situations. She had ignored her critics for the most part. The final straw came when she was turned down for a bank loan to expand her business. It seemed like a good time to step out of her career.

Besides, she had children to raise. Her sleuthing career had quickly faded from view and she didn't miss that life. Those days were long ago and far away. It was absurd to think that she'd ever want any of that back.

Over a decade later, she and her family had hidden from the government under an assumed name—it was a long story that she didn't want to dwell on at that moment. A few months after she went into hiding, her actions seemed foolish and excessive. The nation had begun its recovery from its first nuclear war and hiding from this threat was no longer necessary.

But it was during her off-grid ordeal that Serena had picked up on suspicious events that had been unfolding around her. Naturally she had investigated. The intention had been to learn what was going on so that she could best protect her family. She hadn't been hired by anyone and her sleuthing hadn't been official.

However, she had inadvertently stumbled upon political corruption at a shockingly high level.

This was what had landed her on President Ann Kinji's radar. Serena had intrigued Ann, she had made Ann laugh, she had been a government outsider, and most of all Serena Wilcox couldn't be bought. Ann had trusted her implicitly. In a corrupt world, it was rare to find a true friend. Ann wasn't about to let her go then or now.

Serena let her eyes close. It wouldn't hurt to rest. She realized with a shock that she hadn't had a full night's sleep in over a week. She let her breathing slow.

She reminisced about her journey as a time traveler, before everything turned into madness. Before she had joined GSI Serena was looking forward to hanging up her sleuthing shoes once again. But Ann had enticed her back in the game by offering her time travel adventures.

Project Scarecrow had quickly turned from a glorious dream into a twisted nightmare, from the first mission onward. Even minor setbacks were sour, like when she had almost lost consciousness because Beav forgot to vent the Ruby Red portal for air flow. Something about that incident was important, she told herself.

She drifted. Her legs kicked in a dream-fall spasm. She jerked awake. Then she shut down again. She closed her eyes one last time as her body slumped.

Natalie Buske Thomas

17

Serena opened her eyes. In her befuddled state she thought that she saw the uniformed man she had seen when she was on Ellis Island. She struggled to regain cognizance, but she still saw the man from Ellis Island. Now his face was mere inches from her own.

"She's coming to," he said.

An Irish immigrant, a boy no older than fifteen, leaned in closer. His well-loved violin slid down his arm. He repositioned it by standing up straight and slinging it over his shoulder. "They are looking at Annie Moore and her brother."

Annie was the first immigrant to register at Ellis Island on New Year's Day, 1892. She and her two brothers had been travelling alone, as her parents had already prepared new lives for them in New York. She was only a young teen girl, but she managed to take care of herself and her two younger brothers on the miserable steerage class journey that spanned twelve days, including Christmas.

In celebration of Ellis Island's opening day, Annie had received a ten dollar coin, world-wide attention, and eventually a statue was created in her honor in both her hometown of Cobh, Co. Cork, Ireland and in Ellis Island. All eyes were on Annie at this moment. She would captivate their attention for a long while.

The Irish lad who had helped hide Serena by blocking the crowd's view of her with his luggage and blanket looked wistfully at Annie. He no doubt wished that he had been the first immigrant to step off the ship. All of the action was happening over there. He could at least celebrate on someone else's behalf, he thought.

The uniformed man rose and said, "Thank you, you can go now."

The boy grinned from ear to ear.

"Please, no word of this to anyone." The man pressed a gold coin into the boy's hand. "There, now you too can celebrate your arrival to America."

The boy's eyes widened. He stood stock still with his mouth open. When the man gestured for him to move along he closed his hand over the coin and disappeared into the crowd.

The uniformed man reached down to grasp Serena's upper arms. He strengthened his hold on her. Seconds later the two of them vanished from Ellis Island, unseen by anyone but the Irish lad whose secrecy had been bought.

Serena materialized safely onto a hospital bed in a room that she would later describe to the crew as a luxury suite. The walls were adorned with a velvety design unlike anything she had seen in wallpaper, paint, or plaster. Whatever this was, it was new. The fixtures were novel as well—they appeared to be made of fabric material, which seemed impossible. The overall effect of fiber, instead of metal, plaster or plastic, was warm and amiable.

Serena sat up. "You're the same man I saw before. You're a time traveler?"

He nodded.

"Apparently you got your own data to travel farther back in time than I thought you could go. Why don't you tell me what you want? We can end this cat and mouse game right now."

"You misunderstand."

"I'll be honest—I'm scared. I've fought you all I can, but I can't compete with your technology. It's bad enough that you've been spying on us at work, at home, and everywhere we go. I don't know how you got me back to Ellis Island. Can you at least tell me why you are doing this?"

The man's eyebrows lifted and his eyes reflected kindness.

Serena was confused. Was this man not on the side of the Redheaded Devil? What was going on? Aloud she said, "Please explain to me what has happened."

The man seemed to consider her request before rejecting it. "You must wait."

The door opened. Serena swung her feet over the side of the hospital bed. A

211

wave of dizziness prevented her from any further action. She sat helplessly as three more men entered the spacious room. Their faces were pleasant looking and their clothing was dressy, nonthreatening, and fashionable. The only uniformed man was the one who had taken her from Ellis Island. Serena realized that he was wearing a period piece costume to fit in at Ellis Island, not a uniform from his own time period. His real clothes were probably in the same style as the other men wore.

A man wearing a deep blue shirt, a yellow tie, and a charcoal suit jacket with tails reached for her wrist. Serena let her hand go limp. Why should she fight, what good would it do? She relaxed when she realized that he was checking her pulse.

He said, "You appear to be normalized."

Serena asked, "What do you mean by that?"

"I am referring to your spell. You lost consciousness due to oxygen deprivation. In that state, your brain fired up your most recent history, 1892, New York America. We sent Mason Jar to retrieve you."

"Mason Jar? Is that really his name?"

No one responded.

She said, "Never mind. Thank you for coming for me. Who are you?"

The man in the yellow tie acted as their spokesperson. "We are from ahead of your time window, yes, but we are not who you think we are."

Serena said, "Well, I no longer think you are those people. The men of the future I thought you were are evil, the kind of evil that shows on the outside, in the hollows of the eyes, in the glint of the stare, and in the tightness of the face. It's undeniable. You don't wear that darkness."

"We are from a more advanced time window than the ones you speak of. We

213

too have a vested interest in their progression."

Serena observed that all of them had deep golden brown eyes of the same shade of coffee. All were in a perfect state of fitness, and all were roughly the same height. They looked similar enough to each other that it was difficult to tell them apart. Even their hair was the same shade of chestnut. Only their wardrobes were different. She also reminded herself that she had yet to see any women.

"Yes, you are on the correct train of thought. We have no women. Yes, we are a cloned population."

Serena gasped. "You're telepathic?"

"Yes. Don't be startled. This should not come as a surprise. It is but a short pilgrimage from teleportation to telepathy."

Serena willed herself to calm down. "I can't read your minds, but you can

214

apparently read mine. Please answer my questions then, since you already know what they are." She swept her dark hair behind her shoulders, folded her arms across her chest, and looked expectantly at the man in the yellow tie.

"We are watching the same men as you are. We are also watching you, watching them. We are grateful that you prevented and thereby reversed the depigmentation program. You see here that we are of diverse skin tones. We prefer diversity. We are of the same mind as you."

The men still looked shockingly alike, diverse only in skin color. The man in the yellow tie ignored Serena's stray thought. He continued, "I must warn you. When you leave bread crumbs in the time window, we follow those crumbs to recreate data that predates our archives. We also use your data to repair ours. The

215

men you are afraid of have developed a scorched earth policy, a term that they adopted after…yes, after their time in World War 1.

"You must try not to interrupt me with your thoughts, Serena Wilcox Bridges. Your thoughts are too loud for me to continue. Yes, that is better. Quiet yourself and focus on what I'm saying. Their scorched earth policy has caused the deletion of entire databases. When they have passed through a time window, they destroy it behind them so that no others may follow. We have exhausted ourselves repairing this damage. Your work has benefited us, and for that we are grateful.

"I have an important message for you now. The man you go to for guidance, the man of science, Eduardo, is leading you down the wrong path. No, not deliberately, no. Again, please do not interrupt. He is nonetheless leading you astray. He has dismissed your concern about the World War 1 and the World War 2 time windows melding. On the contrary, you are correct.

"This is the action of sabotage. The men you are running from, while also chasing after, had developed a fixation on the rise and fall of Adolf Hitler. It is their frequent journeys into those decades of Hitler's adulthood that have created the melding of the two wars. No, you need not concern yourself with those wars. I do not mean to mislead you—these men have abandoned their obsession with Hitler. Do not return to that time window. You must stay away from it.

"The awareness I want to impart to you is that the men you fear have indeed forced bubbles to surface in the time window. These bubbles did cause a melding of the two time windows, which did result in anomalies, one of which you had noticed. This melding is inconsequential at present, and on that point your Eduardo is correct. But it alarms us greatly. We disagree with his dismissal of this concern. If anomaly can happen once, it can happen again, and if it does, it may have catastrophic results. We have decided as a collective to get involved.

"We will help you, Serena Wilcox Bridges. Yes, you are correct in thinking that we are pressuring you to accept this help, but you are incorrect in your other thoughts. We will not force our will upon you, or persecute you, or do harm to your people. We are utopia seekers, not oppressors. We do not dominate. We do not control. We do offer you our help, which you and we need.

"To restate the matter: we need the help we wish to give to ourselves, through you. So it is with gravity indeed that I ask for your mercy. Please allow us to assist you."

18

Serena in real time, present day, was missing. The crew waited for her for ten minutes before attempting to contact her through her wrist band. Receiving no response didn't worry them much. She had probably turned it off.

They looked for her in GSI's labyrinth of corridors while Lehman accessed the disabled wristband. It took a while but his persistence paid off when he pulled up her

GPS coordinates. He groaned when he saw the results, assuming that the data was flawed. Then he considered the possibility that the data was correct. If the GPS coordinates placed Serena right there on the GSI landing pad, how was it possible that no one saw her? He ran to the tarmac.

"She's in the pod."

Beav said, "What do you mean by 'the pod'?"

Lehman said, "The thing you built for her. The pod, the portal, whatever you call it. Open it."

Beav remembered the oxygen deprivation glitch. He sprinted to the landing pad and swore under his breath as he struggled to remember the combination for the security code to open Ruby Red's door. He was about to use the iris scanner to open the hatch when it opened up on its own.

"I'm back," said Serena.

Beav said, "You're back? Where were you? I thought you blacked out."

"I did. I need coffee. Do you need coffee? Oh that's right, you abstain from caffeine. I want something to eat. I need red meat. Let's go to a truck stop. They still have truck stops right? We can go to one?"

Beav said, "You're going to the ER."

Serena weaved her way across the landing pad toward the GSI building. "I'm fine."

Agent Estep was exiting GSI as Serena went down. He caught her before she hit the pavement. He grunted, hoisted her over his shoulder, turned around and went back into the building. "I think she's heavier than the last time."

Beav said, "I wouldn't advise telling her that."

Estep stormed through the lobby with Serena's lifeless body. Ruby pressed a

223

button under the counter and said, "Bring her right through there. No, use the other door. Keep going. Help is on the way."

Because a medical team was on staff at GSI, response time was only two minutes. Oxygen was administered, an IV line was initiated, and Serena was hooked up to a monitor. Her temperature was lower than normal and her heart rate was slow, but she was now taking in shallow breaths and her stats improved immediately. Jo relieved Estep from nursing duty, prepared for a long shift. But within minutes Serena was scrabbling at the oxygen mask so that she could talk.

"Stop messing with that! You'll have plenty of time to brief us when you're up to snuff."

Jo's red hair was loose and frizzy. Serena saw a blurry red halo around Jo's face.

"Why are you staring at me like that? Wait, don't answer. Let the oxygen do its job."

Serena closed her eyes. She drifted in and out for the next couple of hours. When she was finally able to stay awake she was surprised to see Tom looking down at her. "Did they let you out early? You didn't quit your job did you?"

Tom said, "Good, you're awake."

Serena tried to sit up. The machines she was connected to bleeped and reported her activity to the monitor. A young doctor ran in.

Tom said, "I was about to come get you."

The doctor checked Serena's vital signs, asked her a few questions, and then spoke to Tom and Jo. "She'll be fine. Let's have her use supplemental oxygen for the rest of the afternoon. She can resume normal activity when she's ready."

Tom asked, "How long was she out for?"

"I doubt that she was unconscious for more than a few minutes. Let her rest for a day or two and she'll be right as rain."

Jo left when the doctor did, after promising Tom that she would instruct the crew to leave them alone. Tom thanked her and then turned his attention to his wife, who already looked significantly better. "Do you want anything?"

"I'm hungry."

"I can get you something."

"No, I want to go home." Serena sat up and swung her legs over the bed. She wasn't dizzy anymore.

"Are you sure?" Tom looked around him, hoping that the doctor would materialize. He did, after Serena unplugged herself from the monitor.

"I want to go home," she said.

The doctor agreed. As long as Tom kept an eye on her there was no reason for her to stay. Serena asked for Beav before she left. "I have a lot to fill you in on. Any chance you're willing to ride home with us to hear it?"

19

Beav listened to Serena without interruption. She described every moment of her encounter with the men from the "future beyond". But she was wearing down now.

"I feel old," she said. "I hate this feeling. I need to make a change."

"Then do it! Do it," said Beav.

"I can't. Tom went back to school to get his master's degree. We have medical bills. We need GSI right now."

"I know. I have responsibilities—people who rely on me. I've thought about making a change too. When I do, I'm making a commitment to it," said Beav.

"Meanwhile here we are. One foot in front of the other," she said.

"What do you want me to do?"

"I need some time to pull myself together. It's not this oxygen deprivation scare, it's not that. I have to let go of what happened between me and the Redheaded Devil. I can't stop thinking about how he looked at me. He wanted me erased. It wasn't enough for me to die. He wanted my kind scrubbed from all eternity. I need to process that."

"Ann has already asked about you. She wants you back by next week."

"I'm fine with that."

"So you only need a few days then?" Beav noticed that the van was slowing. Tom had pulled into their neighborhood.

"Yes, a few days are plenty. I want you to work on something while I'm out."

"You want me to find the Redheaded Devil?"

Serena looked at him with surprise. "Isn't that what we've been doing?"

"It is."

"And you haven't heard back from the lab yet?"

"Not yet. I'll call when I do."

Serena said, "There's not much to do with that then."

Tom pulled the van into the family's garage. Beav said, "You're going to have to spell it out for me. What do you want me to do?"

"We got our color back, but the men of the future are still cloning. There are no women, no children, no elderly and no

231

disabled persons. There's a long way to go."

Tom got out of the van and went into the house. Serena assured him that she wouldn't be long. Beav and Serena stayed in the garage to wrap up their conversation.

Beav said, "I'll have to give this a long think. Unless you've got some ideas?"

"You'll have to look into cloning research."

Beav snapped his fingers. "I don't know why I didn't think of that. I'll bring Eduardo, make a speech, and get them to back off their research. That formula worked smashingly the first time around."

"It could work," said Serena.

"It will, it will." Beav got out of the van. "I'm going to take off. Estep is meeting me a few blocks from here."

"Do you want Tom to give you a lift?"

"No, I could use a run."

Serena waved him off and went into the house. Beav made sure that she was greeted inside before leaving. All appeared to be well. He was optimistic that Serena would be back on the job even sooner than she expected.

Meanwhile, Agent Estep was probably already at the pub. Not that he was drinking, he never drank while on call. Come to think of it, Beav questioned if Estep ever took a drink. Was he ever not on call?

Beav felt refreshed after his short run. He was going to beat himself up in the gym when this mission was over. It'd been too long. His legs shouldn't be on fire.

He entered the pub and searched for Estep, expecting to find him sitting here, glaring at the door. He wasn't. Beav made his way to the back of the pub, but there was still no sign of Estep. He checked the restroom. Empty. Clearly he wasn't in the

233

building. Now, if this was anyone else, Beav would have assumed that his friend was running late. But this was Estep. Something was off. Beav put in a call and got no answer. Next he called GSI.

Ruby answered, "Is that you, Beav?"

"It is I."

"You better come in."

20

Ann Kinji and Ruby met Beav in the vacant lobby. He'd never seen the building so quiet. His heart raced when he smelled copper. Then he saw the blood, the buckets and buckets of blood.

"They're all gone," said Ann.

Beav felt his own blood drain from his face. His legs barely held him up. "All of them? How? What happened?"

Ann stared at him. "You look sick. Are you OK?"

Beav was taken aback. "Are *you* OK?"

Ann realized what he must have thought. "Oh, no, no. They aren't dead. The GSI teams are all out. They went after the Redheaded Devil after he did this to us."

"What is this? I'm seeing blood. Is this not blood?" Beav added, "A *lot* of blood."

Ann sighed. "Yes, it's blood. They stabbed a pig. They left it lying there on the floor. Poor wretched thing. They left it there to die with the knife still in it."

Ruby handed Beav a blood-stained piece of paper. She said, "This was between the blade and the pig."

Beav skimmed the note as fast as his eyes could move. "I know what you did. You think you can change us, think again. This time it's a pig. Next time, it's you. All of you. Starting with that shrew."

Ann took the note from him. "This is evidence. We shouldn't have handled it."

Beav said, "And everyone's gone looking for the MOTF? Why? What do they hope to gain from this? Do they have a plan?"

Ann said, "Estep ran off with his Special Forces team. I didn't know anything about this until he had already left. Lehman normally loops me in, but he's in the air on his way home. Remember he's already extended his time here."

Beav took a bandana out of his pocket and knotted it on his head. "I'll go in after him. But what about Buick? Why didn't he put a stop to this?"

Ann said, "Buick's home too. With Serena out, it seemed a good time to let the crew take some down time. Estep was the last one here, except for me and Ruby. He was on his way out to meet somebody."

"Yeah, me. He was supposed to meet with me. I got no call, nothing. We were going to go over what Serena told me."

Ann said, "What can I say? No one was here to stop him. You know how he is. Find out what he's up to. There's nothing I can do until I know what's going on."

Beav said, "Agreed. Let's not panic. Estep has a highly trained team with him. He's got it under control. Come to think of it, I wonder if I shouldn't use this distraction to our advantage."

Ann said, "How so?"

Beav said, "Hmm, I can talk to you about that later."

He headed down the corridor toward his hall of mirrors. Ann waited a few minutes and then went the opposite direction until she made her way back to the same place. She found Beav in the safe room. "I wish we could speak freely," she said. "Meeting in the storage closet has become tiresome."

"I know, but this is the best we can do for now. About Estep, I meant what I said. I'm confident that he has this. I'm better off going on the mission Serena proposed."

"Which is?"

"She wants me to stop cloning research." Beav studied Ann's face and he didn't like what he saw in her expression. "What? You don't approve?"

Ann said, "It's too late."

"Meaning?"

"It's classified."

Beav whistled. "I see. Well, I can go back in time and stop them before it got this far along."

Ann said, "It's complicated."

"I don't see what choice we have. Women will be wiped out in the future through cloning run amok."

239

"Cloning research has found a cure for many types of cancer. There is new progress toward a cure for autism, multiple sclerosis, lupus, diabetes and so much more. How can we take this away from people?"

Beav said, "I don't feel comfortable making this decision."

Ann said, "Neither do I."

Suddenly a voice from the doorway called out, "Rock, paper, scissors?"

"Serena! What are you doing here?" Beav asked.

Ann said, "Sorry, I called her as soon as Estep left. I know I said I'd let her take some time off, but obviously she's needed." She addressed Serena, "You're functioning well enough, aren't you?"

"Tip top. I caught the end of your conversation. How about this? We create a powerful ethics committee to oversee the cloning research. We'll know if our plan works or not. All we have to do is set this plan in motion, and then visit our futuristic travelers. If nothing has changed, we failed."

Ann said, "Sounds reasonable. Consider it done."

"Really, that fast?" Serena asked.

"I was the president. It carries weight. I only have to delegate this with a phone call. From there, the wheels will churn slowly, but if what I set in motion works, you'll see the results. Give me a couple of hours, then go."

Beav said, "Estep may have already found the MOTF, but if not, how do you propose we find our futuristic travelers? And which ones should we track down? The good ones or the bad ones?"

Serena said, "Whichever ones we find first."

Natalie Buske Thomas

21

Ann had left for her meeting, multi-tasking along the way. As promised, she delegated the task of creating a cloning ethics committee in less than two hours. This committee was to be a supreme entity, to supersede the committee they already had.

An ethics committee had been in place from day one, but had obviously been proven by future events to be woefully inadequate. Ann proposed stricter guidelines, consequences if researchers broke the rules, and two internal affairs investigators assigned to every team of scientists to hold everyone accountable. Furthermore, this new regulation was to be paid for by taxing pharmaceutical, medical supply, and other businesses. Any corporation or private investor who profited from cloning research would pay an ethics tax.

Ann was proud of these ideas, but there was no guarantee that her proposal would make it through the red tape to implementation. If her proposal succeeded, Beav and Serena would see the evidence of that when they find the MOTF.

After Ann left, Beav and Serena ruminated. Of concern was what, if anything, the MOTF would do to sabotage Ann's proposal. Surely they were watching and listening. However, the Redheaded

Devil hadn't prevented Eduardo from discontinuing the depigmentation research project. Perhaps the MOTF were limited in how much they could do. There was nothing that GSI could do about the laws of the universe. Serena suggested that they stop focusing on what they can't control, and focus on what they can.

Beav stood in the center of the safe room closet with his arms folded across his chest. His bowed his head. His bandana slipped but didn't fall off. "I'm thinking."

Serena said, "I can see that."

Beav continued, "I'm thinking that we should split up. You've already met the men of the distant future. It doesn't make sense that I should look for them. And it's my turn to save Agent Estep. You got him last time around."

"Fair enough. I'll go my way, and you go yours. Do you have any idea where either of those places are?"

Beav said, "That's why I'm thinking."

The two stood in silence for a few agonizingly long minutes. Serena started to say something and then stopped herself. Beav said, "What? Spill it."

"You can track Estep, right? Can't you find him through his band?"

"Of course. I know where I'm going. But where are we sending you?"

"I'm getting to my idea, bear with me. Past events are recorded too, right?"

"Yes…"

"So then, you can backtrack to find out where I was when I was with the men in the distant future, when they had me in their own world."

"In the future."

"Yes, when they brought me there. Except that I didn't have the band, and it wasn't programmed by you. This was teleportation through one of them. So, I'm not sure there's any data for you to track."

246

"Yes, that's what I've been pondering. I don't know if they left any code in your brain and there's only one way to find out." Beav stared at her head.

"Oh dear," said Serena.

"Yes, dear."

"All right. I'm willing. What do you have to do? Do you have to shave my head?"

Beav laughed. "No, nothing like that. It's simple, painless, and you won't even know I've extracted anything from you."

"Then why all the pondering?"

"The hard part is how I'm going to sort the data once I have it. I was configuring imaginary data."

"Put Nicholas, Lehman, and all of our best IT people on it. You shouldn't have to do this yourself."

"Agreed, but Ann expected us to zip out of here. This is going to take time. And the more people know about this, the less chance of keeping it a secret. Meanwhile, who knows what Estep is dealing with."

"Like you said before, he has a military team with him."

Beav suddenly punched his fist into his other hand, making Serena jump. "Got it!"

"Yes?"

"It was the last place you traveled, right? You went nowhere else?"

"GSI was the last place."

"Home base doesn't count. Besides GSI, was it the last place you traveled?"

"Yes."

Beav shouted, "Eureka!"

"You can find the last place visited?"

"Yes indeedy, my friend!"

"How long will this take?"

Beav pretended to look at his watch. "How do you feel about now?"

22

Beav was careful not to cross time windows with Serena. He let her leave first, then he waited twenty minutes before leaving to find Estep. Time travel generally wasn't instantaneous as most people expected it to be. Beav thought of it as buffering. What should be instant wasn't always. Sometimes there was a delay. One mission had caused them to be frozen in time for nearly fifteen minutes. That was a harrowing experience! Planning for glitches was imperative. His planning paid off. The travel was well-executed, uneventful, and landed him directly in front of Agent Estep.

Estep jolted backward a good five feet. He yelled, "Don't ever do that again!"

Beav didn't reply. He was too preoccupied with studying his surroundings. "What's all this? And where is everybody? I thought you had the Xtreme team with you."

Estep said, "I dismissed them."

"Why? What's going on?" Beav tried to guess what had happened but his mind was a blank.

"Are you going to let me explain or are you going to ask me more questions?"

Beav rubbed the back of his neck. "Explain. Make it fast, we might have a problem." He looked at the walls and fixtures. All of the décor was covered with ornate textiles. Something about this room was vaguely familiar.

Estep said, "I was running down a lead."

"And?" Beav prodded. "If you don't want me to interrupt you, don't stop talking. Let's start with what I know. You found the stuck pig and the threatening note. You stormed off after the Redheaded Devil. Am I right so far? Where did you go? Where are we now? How did you know where to find him?"

"That's what I was saying. Mandolin knew where he was. He was following him."

Beav felt like he was running in circles. "What does Mandolin have to do with this? He was here?"

Estep scuffed the toe of his boot along the floor. He exhaled noisily. "No. Mandolin was sitting outside GSI. The

251

MOTF were staking us out. I got him there, at home."

"And? Tell me the whole story."

"I got to him, and he snapped off. He said I'd never get him because there were too many of him. He was starting to go and I grabbed him. He brought me with him to his world. I was sucked in along with him."

"The Xtreme team too?"

"No. I dismissed them before that."

"Why would you do that?" Beav struggled to nail down what happened and the order in which it occurred.

"I don't use them in civilian operations. The MOTF were in our city, on our streets. It's a jurisdiction issue of sorts."

"Got it. So, OK then, you ended up alone with them in their world."

"No."

"No?"

"I landed there, on top of him. I messed him up, my two-hundred plus goodness on his head. He wasn't moving."

Beav's eyes twinkled. "He's dead?"

"Don't get too excited. He was still breathing last I saw him. He won't be down long."

"So where is he?" Beav asked.

"In his world, wherever that is." Estep tapped his foot. He glanced at the doorway.

Beav looked around him, as if expecting the walls to talk. "That's not where we are now?"

"No. I told you."

"No, you didn't tell me. You're infuriating, you know that, Estep? Where are we?"

"I saw that the Devil was under me. I stood up and the next thing I knew I was somewhere else. They told me to wait

253

here." Estep's eyes tracked movement at the door.

"Who's they?" asked Beav.

He pointed at the three men who entered the room. "Them."

The men gathered around. Beav didn't see any sign of joy on their faces. "We failed, didn't we?"

They shook their heads in unison. One of them said, "You did not fail, but you did not succeed."

Beav sighed. "After pulling my hair out from trying to extract information from Agent Estep, I have no patience left for deciphering riddles. My guess is that you are the men that our Serena Wilcox saw in what she called the 'distant' future. Your time window is beyond the MOTF. We call you the good guys. *Are* you the good guys? Enlighten us please. Do you know everything about us? Are we ants in an ant farm to you? What do you want

254

from us? Tell us everything we need to know. Let's cut to the chase here."

One of them said, "We are not chasing you. We mean you no harm."

Beav said, "I see that we have a language barrier of some kind. That's not what I meant. What I'm trying to say is that I want you to teach us about you. Please tell us how we're connected. What do you know about us? Why are we important to you? What do you want from us? You there, you're wearing a yellow tie. Did you meet Serena Wilcox?"

The man with the yellow tie stepped forward. "Yes, I told her what we want from you. Did she not give you a report?"

Beav nodded. "She did. Now please tell me more."

The man in the yellow tie turned to the other two and dismissed them. He indicated that Beav and Estep should sit in the chairs by the faux hearth. He sat with them. Then he spoke in an unhurried manner, and continued to talk for several minutes, as if he had prepared a speech in anticipation of this occasion.

"You did not fail in your quest to curtail the cloning experiments. Research did continue, however, on its intended path toward medical discoveries that benefit the future of humanity. You could not destroy the research in its entirety as inhibiting it would have meant the loss of thousands of lives. We are in agreement with that course.

You had also succeeded in thwarting the one-gendered path and the genetic selection of the most ideal zygotes. All of that did go according to your plan. The difficulty arose when we could not find room for all members of the population. Without genetic selection and limitation, we became too populous. Even with the implantation of severe fertility restrictions, we could not contain the inhabitants. We exceeded capacity."

Beav said, "How can it be that there is not enough space? Are you not utilizing land efficiently? Haven't you made technological advances to make use of formerly uninhabitable areas? Even in my time we have made great gains in this area."

The man stared without blinking. He said, "We have. We created this." He indicated the four walls. "This is what we have."

Estep asked, "Do you mean that there is no outside environment? Are we on a ship?"

The man finally blinked his eyes. Then he kept them closed while he spoke. "No, we are not on a ship. We are in a terrarium pod. We have hundreds of pods, but we cannot produce more of them. We have not enough materials to maintain additional pods without mining the environment beyond our resources. We are finite. We must control our population growth."

Beav said, "So I'm to assume then that the outside world is uninhabitable. Why? What happened to it? Nuclear war? Global warming? How did we ruin the planet?"

"We aren't on a planet."

Estep said, "I knew it! We're on a ship."

"No. I told you. We are in a terrarium pod."

Beav said, "If not on a planet, where are we?"

"We have lived for fourteen years on this colony. We journeyed here after the space exploration boom."

Estep said, "Are we on the sun? Why haven't we burned up?"

"The sun is a star. You are close in your understanding."

Estep said, "So we're on a star then?"

"If you can grasp that scientists found a celestial body that does not fit the definition of either a planet or a star, you can then open your mind to imagine yet another classification, that doesn't fit the known criteria. While astronomers have learned basic facts about celestial bodies, there is more to be discovered than can ever be known.

Stars emit light on their own, while planets do not. Stars are a large collection of plasma with a nuclear reactor at their core. How then can we live here, with temperatures as high as the sun? We cannot live on a star confined by that narrow definition, not even in a terrarium pod. We can, however, live on the newly formed celestial bodies that were born in the space of my generation.

These bodies do emit light on their own, but they are not quite stars or planets,

259

and yet not brown dwarfs either. They are a new kind of celestial body never before seen."

Estep says, "It's close enough to a star to me."

The man stared at Estep, tilted his head to the side like a bird analyzing his situation. He said, "You can refer to it as a star if you wish, while I insist that you are incorrect in doing so. However, you are correct about our advancements in technology. We did find ways to make previously uninhabitable places habitable. What you did not imagine is that new types of 'stars' were born that are unlike any you have in your time. I have explained that these new bodies do emit light, which classifies them as closer to stars than planets. But their core temperature is much cooler. Nonetheless, the conditions are not ideal.

While we can colonize here, we cannot live outside of a terrarium pod. Therefore, our exits are protected by a sally port. Because we cannot leave the pod we rely heavily on teleportation and time travel."

Estep said, "You're prisoners."

"No. We can teleport into any time window we desire. We can choose to give up our citizenship here. We can petition to return to Planet Earth, or elsewhere."

Beav said, "There's an 'elsewhere'?"

"Yes. But I must not tell you more than you need to know."

Estep said, "Why did you leave? What's wrong with Earth?"

"We left for a variety of reasons. This is the end of your inquiries."

Beav said, "But we still don't know what our role is in all of this. You said that we succeeded in reversing ethnic cleansing but we failed to bring the female gender back from extinction. Does this apply to Earth as well, or is population control only an issue for star colonists? What do you want with us?"

"We shouldn't have ever come."

Estep said, "It's too late now, you've brought us here. You may as well tell us what you want."

"No, you misunderstand. I meant that our people should never have colonized this body you call a star. We have named this place SpicaAlcor, meaning 'the bright one, the neglected one'. We should never have colonized beyond our planet. We should not have expanded our habitation of the universe. We should not have taken for ourselves more than what was granted to us."

Beav said, "You haven't told us what the problem is. Are you in trouble? I'm doing my best to keep up with all that you are saying. I haven't heard you mention any reason for us to be here, and I'm not seeing any signs of danger."

"I shall bring you understanding. We have modified humanity, this you have witnessed for yourself. We have no young, no old, and no females. Furthermore we have cloned ourselves for maximum longevity. We have eliminated features that are not efficient. We do not laugh or smile because our faces do not require those commands to survive. We are energy efficient. We engineered our bodies to sustain us with fewer energy requirements, do you understand?"

Beav frowned. "Yes, I think that I do. I take it that you remember a time when you did laugh and smile, and you once knew women?"

"No. I do not know these things firsthand. I know them from my travels into the past. I have seen what we are not. I have learned that we are not altogether

263

human. We are people, but we are not human. We breathe and we function. We do not feel. We do not know love. We do not know happiness. We know of these things only from observation and research. These things were stolen from us."

Estep said, "Stolen how? Who did this to you?"

"The one you call the Redheaded Devil did this to us. It is his generation who took cloning to unprecedented heights. It is his generation that birthed the astronomers who discovered new stars. It is his generation that planned the first terrarium pods."

Estep said, "He's already a target. We'll get him."

"You must disrupt the politics of his day. You must make certain that no one else will rise to his position. The entire political climate must be shut down. They must be made to understand that colonization is a dark path that leads to this, to what we are. We cannot live where we do not belong without becoming less than human. You must stop them from doing this to us. Please. We know what we have lost. We have seen it, in you, in others. We have watched humans live. We have watched them love. We have watched them die. We know that we are not human. But you mustn't fear us. We lack the capacity for anger. We cannot hurt you. Emotional response is not in our genetic code. But we are cognitive of what we are, and we have an intellectual capacity to qualify what we are missing. We can define humanity. We can desire that which is optimal. We can comprehend what is good and what is evil. We are neither good nor evil, nor do we feel that one or the other is right or wrong, but we have analyzed that evil has made us what we are. Our conclusion is that evil is 'wrong', even though we do not have what you might refer to as a moral conscience."

Estep said, "You talk in a robotic way. Are you cyborgs?"

"No, we are genetically optimized humans. I apologize for my stilted manner of speaking. American English is not my native tongue. My words are auto-translated. I speak a hybrid of Arabic and British English, known as Abe. It was developed by the World Order as a universal language and adopted by the council. Education reform required that all children be taught Abe. This movement toward a one-language world is not of your concern. We do not ask you to interfere with this event. I have said too much. I mean only to ask for you to stop the march toward colonization before it begins."

Estep said, "Auto-translated? Then you are part robot."

The man said, "No. We wear embedded chips to make computer tasks more efficient, the same as you. Your generation has early stages of these chips, mainly for tracking purposes. We carry mini computers with us. This does not make us cyborgs, no more than it makes you a cyborg. Are you not wearing a GPS locator chip at this moment?"

Beav said, "Maybe I'm being obtuse, but why don't you just go back to Earth?"

The man said, "It is too late for us to reverse this colonization. Many of them do not know any other way. They do not travel and they cannot understand that they are not fully human."

Estep turned to Beav. "I wish Serena was hearing this. Why didn't she come with you?"

Beav's eyes flew open. "Serena! Where is she? She was looking for your people, here I presume. Why isn't she here?"

"Did she attempt travel at the same time as you?" the man asked.

Beav said, "No, I specifically waited for her to go first, then I came later."

The man looked at Estep. "You then? Did she leap at the same time that you were traveling?"

Estep looked at Beav. "I don't know. Did she? Is that how I got here? Did we trade places then? I thought that you people brought me here."

The man shook his head. "No. We didn't summon your arrival. You merely appeared."

Beav said, "So if you're here, and Serena's where you were, that means she's with the Redheaded Devil."

23

Serena landed hard. That was her first clue that materialization had gone wrong. Her second clue was that she was sitting on top of somebody. She realized that wires were crossed when she recognized who that someday was.

The Redheaded Devil wasn't stirring, but he was moaning. She knew he'd be conscious soon. She sprang to her feet and walked the room. She looked high and low,

269

listened at each of the three doorways—all of the doors were closed and there were no sounds coming from the other side of the doors. No one else was in the area, at least for now.

She looked at her nemesis lying on the floor and she knew what she had to do. It was up to her to take this man out. If she didn't, he would hurt millions of people. She was no killer and she had no appetite for violence, but she never shrank from doing what needed to be done. This needed to be done.

Serena prayed. Afterwards her resolve was even stronger. If she had misunderstood what God wanted, surely He'd forgive her. No, there was no other way out. The opportunity had come to her, and therefore the responsibility was hers. She could do nothing, or she could end this right now. But she had to act fast. He was waking up.

He bolted upright. "What are *you* doing here?"

Serena backed away from him. She said, "I'm probably going to kill you. Do you need a moment?"

The Devil cackled and flicked his tongue. "What do you think you can do?" He got up on his knees.

"I hope you're preparing to pray. If I were you, I'd beg for my soul."

The Devil spat at her, barely missing her head. He lurched to his feet but was unsteady. He moved toward her with his arms outstretched. His red hair flailed in a current of static electricity.

"Before you expire, you never did tell me why you have a forked tongue."

The Devil flicked his tongue and smacked his lips with it. "I wanted it this way. I have a tattoo too. Want to see it?" He tore at the buttons on his shirt. He flung his shirt across the room. His chest

271

lain bare, a tattoo of a serpent sprawled across his flesh. The serpent's head included a black head of hair. On the snake's face was a small black square mustache.

Serena stared at the tattoo until she understood what she was seeing. Then she drew in a sharp breath and exhaled quickly. "That's it, your time is up." She activated her time travel course back to the GSI landing pad. She positioned herself within three feet of the Devil.

His eyes grew round with realization. "I know what you're doing!" He reached out to grab her, but it was too late.

24

Serena was prepared for a hideous sight upon landing on the tarmac. She was relieved that nothing truly gruesome transpired. The Redheaded Devil simply vaporized. Nothing was left but a pile of clothes and his red hair.

She relaxed too soon. From the pile of clothes a flash of movement caught her eye. The Devil's forked tongue had somehow survived beyond the rest of his body and was slithering about, darting fast along the ground as if it were a snake. Serena didn't scream. She froze for half a second before she flew into action. She raced for Ruby Red's iris scanner, opened her left eye wide until the hatch opened, leaned inside the portal and felt for the trowel someone had left in her dead flower garden. She ran back to the pile of clothes.

The Devil's tongue was now zipping madly about. It honed in on Serena and darted straight for her. She held the trowel in both hands like a baseball bat. She waited for the snake-like tongue to reach her feet. She told her herself, you have one shot. She raised the trowel over her head and slammed it onto the pavement.

And then she started screaming. Material from the tongue had splatted her from head to toe. She threw down the trowel and ran around in circles, wringing her hands and screeching until the doors of GSI burst open.

Jo stared at the pavement. "What is that thing?" Serena's hot coal dance hadn't slowed. Jo yelled, "Stop running!"

Serena stopped. "Get it off me, get it off me!"

Jo looked her up and down. "Eew, what is that gunk all over you? Is it from that thing?"

"Just get it off me!"

"OK, let's go inside." GSI maintained a small gym for staff use, but it and the accompanying shower room were on the top floor. GSI staff had been called in to help. They were now coming out in droves to watch Serena go up the escalator. They didn't even wait until she was out of earshot before speculating about why she was covered in goo.

Jo found Serena's locker and retrieved her gym bag. She found a pair of clean sweat pants, a T-shirt and a pair of tennis shoes. There were no socks, but she could do without those. Jo helped Serena peel off her damp clothes, doing her best to avoid letting any of the goo touch Serena's skin. "I assume you don't want to keep these," she said.

"Bag them up for evidence."

"Right." Jo found a fresh garbage bag and dropped Serena's clothes into it. "OK, I'll make sure the water's warm, then I'll leave you to it. Or should I stay? You're not dizzy or anything, are you? I don't want you falling and hitting your head."

"No, I'm fine. I can get the water myself. Gather everyone up in the safe room. Oh, and you should get someone to clean up that mess—tell them to scrape it all into an evidence bag."

Serena took her time in the shower. She scrubbed with soap over and over again. She imagined the goo on her skin, even though it may not have ever touched her body under her clothes. She showered until there was no soap left.

She entered the safe room with wet hair, dressed in her gym clothes. She was greeted with awe. Estep said, "You got him. Congratulations."

The crew applauded.

Ann Kinji said, "We'll put you in for honors and a promotion."

Serena looked at her. "Are you serious? I just want to go home."

No one spoke. This wasn't the reaction they had expected from her.

Beav said, "You asked us to meet."

Serena said, "Yes, let's get the debrief over with. I killed the Redheaded Devil by sucking him into my teleportation. We'll no doubt learn how this affects the balance of the universe later. That's really all I have to say. You can analyze the evidence and compare it to what the lab already has."

Beav said, "We have a lot to tell you though. Estep and I…"

Serena cut him off. "Record it. Send me the clip. I'm going home."

They watched her leave and waited to make sure that she wasn't coming back. Then Estep said, "She's going to quit, isn't she?"

Ann shook her finger like an angry school teacher. "I won't let that happen."

Beav said, "I think I can persuade her to stay on with GSI if you agree to let her work from home. We don't need her here. Anything we have to share with her can be teleconferenced. When she's scheduled for a mission she'll teleport from her living room. The tarmac has never been for anything more than show."

Ann said, "Security concerns?"

Beav said, "We can't use this storage closet forever anyway. Eventually we'll have to do business as usual. When

Lehman gets back he's going to help us find the bugs. We can figure this out. Let her work from home. Trust me, you're going to lose her otherwise."

Ann capitulated. "I'll draw up a new contract for her."

"Good. I'm glad that's settled," said Beav. "I'll fill you in on what Estep and I know, and then I'm off to the lab. They say they have the results of the DNA testing for the Redheaded Devil, although the urgency of this seems moot at this point."

Natalie Buske Thomas

25

Mandolin rang the doorbell and waited for Serena Wilcox to appear. He looked for her eyes in the stained glass window of the foyer door. He saw only the top of her head. He had forgotten how short she was.

Serena had been expecting him, but even so, it was odd to see Mandolin at her house. She let him in. She offered him a cup of coffee and an oatmeal cookie. He

281

accepted both offerings. He let the small talk run its natural course before he approached the business at hand. "They want me here to protect you."

Serena said, "Hmm. I'm aware."

He leaned across the table and lowered his voice. "I can be more than a bodyguard."

Serena was flustered. She looked around for Tom or the kids to appear. Why was she alone with Mandolin at her kitchen table, she asked herself.

Mandolin laughed until his great belly shook. One of his gold teeth sparkled every time his mouth opened. He let out one last guffaw before he settled down. "It's not what you think. I can be more to you professionally. The GSI teams move too slow. That Devil will get you unless you get him first."

Serena said, "Finding him will be a challenge. The lab said that the DNA results indicate that the Redheaded Devil was born in a petri dish. And the DNA results from the, uh, fragments and specimens on the tarmac differ from the DNA lifted from the previous two samples. They say he has cloned himself at least once and I can only claim one dead body. He's still out there. If he's cloned himself multiple times we'll never be rid of him. I don't see a way out of this. He knows that we've been after him. He probably makes more of himself to keep up."

Mandolin slid his wooden chair across the floor and walked away from the table. "Come with me."

"No. I'm staying here."

Mandolin sat back down. "Alright then. I was going to take you to my cousin's farm so you could see for yourself. He has these crazy birds that live off of ticks. He doesn't feed these things. They go around the house eating bugs. They're nasty looking things, heads like turkeys. He's got this one rooster who stands there with his mouth open. I asked what that dude was doing. My cousin says 'watch'. He stood there, doing nothing but leaving his beak open. He was downwind from the bees. That lazy bird stood there and sure enough those stupid bees flew straight into his mouth! He got himself a regular feast."

Serena imagined this scene. "Are you making this up?"

Mandolin crossed his heart with his fingers. "You'd have seen it with your own eyes if you'd let me take you there."

"And your point is? You think the Redheaded Devil will come to us if we sit here with our beaks wide open?"

"Look, chica, if you go to him, you'll be ambushed. You don't know how many clones he's made. If you wait around for GSI you're a sitting duck. I can get him to come to us. I'll be here with my beak wide open. No matter how many bees come this way, they'll all fly straight into my trap."

"My kids are here."

Mandolin tapped his fingers on the table. "Yeah, I know."

Serena shook her head. "I shouldn't have ever joined GSI."

"Hey now, don't talk like that. We'll get him. I saw a feature about you a while back. You were number twenty-one on a list of kick-ass heroines. You have a reputation, chica."

Serena laughed.

"There we go. I've got your back. Is it true that you've been earning belts in marital arts?"

"I've been taking classes."

Mandolin snorted. "I don't have much use for that myself. I have all I need here…" He pulled his hands into fists.

"And here." He thumped the handle of the gun protruding from his pocket.

26

Eduardo addressed the GSI staff, Special Forces teams, the military cabinet, former President Ann Kinji, and current President Joseph Smythe. He couldn't hold his hands steady. His mustache pulling was uncoordinated enough that several of the generals assumed that Eduardo had taken a nip of something before his presentation.

Eduardo began awkwardly, without any introduction to speak of. He launched immediately into his lecture. "Global positioning systems utilize the spacetime curvature. What were only abstract mathematical equations in 1916 are now routinely used in a tangible way that all of us can understand. When time travel first pioneered, it was not much of a leap forward, given that technology was already utilizing the spacetime curvature. We as a progressive society accepted the new technology without difficulty. I dare say we even embraced the new frontier.

Science moves ever forward. The study of the subatomic world, particle physics, is a quest to decipher the language of nature. I believe that particle physics combined with our rather primitive studies of the genome, as well as advancements in infertility treatments have been instrumental in the progress of cloning research and technology. Slowing this down is not in our best interests, in my humble opinion, nor is it fully possible. However, we are not the only persons making such advances and critical decisions that impact all of humankind.

I turn your attention now to the diagram I've placed before you in hologram form. Space-time warpage involves the addition of quantum theory to the theory of relativity. With this combination, time can behave like another dimension of space. We have seen evidence of this, as our traveling companions have crossed into our world and we have crossed into theirs.

Always at some measure of comfort has been the idea that if a scientific theory is correct, it can predict what we'll find if we look in a certain place, in a certain way, at a certain time. But we scientists aren't soothsayers or oracles. We don't predict the future. We merely discover, or put an understanding to things that are already there.

Unfortunately, the ability to predict the outcome implies the ability to *control* the outcome, and nothing could be further from the truth. So while we do predict that cloning research will result in unintended consequences, we can't control that eventuality—the known outcome involving the genetic cleansing and optimizing that will one day occur—nor can we do much to slow that train down.

Nonetheless, there is much we can do. Physicist Frank Oppenheimer worked on the atomic bomb, and yet while it seems contradictory, he was of the belief that 'goodie drops' were far more effective than bombs. He said that social interventions were well behind science. We'd do better to bribe our enemies by dropping food on them instead of bombs. Let this sink in,

Gentlemen of the War Cabinet. Can you anticipate where my lecture is headed?

We've engaged, antagonized, and even killed our enemy. And yet the female gender remains eradicated. Genetic optimization was not thrown off course. Colonization of stars occurred as scheduled. Nothing changed, other than the resurgence of minor racial variations resulting in differences in skin tones. Facial features and body types were for the most part largely identical to the cloned physique we first documented here at the Göbel Solutions Institute.

It is my personal recommendation then, that we entice our enemies to comply with our demands by bribery, by social intervention. This path of action will be far more effective than any war we could declare upon them."

Eduardo's speech had a lukewarm reception. Only half the room applauded.

291

The military was having none of it, and the GSI staff was split down the middle. It was impossible to guess what either Ann or President Joe were thinking as each had developed remarkable poker faces—mainly from playing actual poker.

Beav stepped up to the podium next. He said, "I'm of a different point of view from Eduardo. Normally I'd call for social intervention, but in this case, the egos of all concerned won't allow it. I don't have any confidence that the men of the future will accept our bribe, any more than I trust their word if they did accept.

First and foremost, we need to locate the original genetics program that manufactured these men. They had an artificial womb initially. When they reached adult age, they were then cloned. Generations thereafter were cloned directly. But prior to that, these men were living much the same as we do. They were born as babies, raised as children, and then they grew into adults.

The only one of them we've had any real contact with is the man we call the Redheaded Devil. We need to find him and trace him back to his petri dish. We need to destroy the entire lab and all others built around that same time. This should remove every manifestation of him that came afterward, except for any manifestations that happen to be traveling somewhere along the time curve at the precise moment of destroying his existence.

I know that this is a drastic measure. I love peaceful outcomes more than anyone, but you should have seen those men on the terrarium pod. Their eyes! My heart bled for them. They begged us to let them be human. Isn't that what freedom is all about?

I believe that humanity will continue as it always has, if we stop the cloning abuse at the moment it first went off course. We're at risk of losing humanity altogether. Isn't that the greatest form of oppression? Well, I'll leave you to your consciences.

Before you go, I encourage you to examine the facial reconstruction models I've brought with me today. My production team put forth a quality effort to give you a reasonable representation of what the Redheaded Devil probably looked like at various stages of his life. Should you vote to approve what I strongly feel is a humanitarian operation, you'll need to know who you're looking for. We don't have a name yet."

Beav received the other half of Eduardo's applause. Like in so many other issues, the room was divided by ideology and politics. Beav was itching to return to

GSI, but first he was expected to hang around and answer any questions. When the Q&A had finally sputtered out he was on his way.

He arrived at the GSI lobby just as Ruby was picking up the phone to call him. "Good, you're back. They're asking if you're ready to go."

"Go?" Beav had nothing on the schedule. He intended to hide away in his office with one of the three books he was in the process of reading.

Ruby sat up straighter in her chair. It wasn't often she that was the first person to know something important. "Didn't they tell you? They voted immediately after the presentation. You got the approval. They want you to find those labs and take them out."

"And what of the Redheaded Devil if he should turn up?"

Ruby made a slicing gesture at her neck.

27

The crew, except for Beav, hit the coffee maker for another round.

They geared up and joined the Xtreme team on the tarmac. Even though Beav had dropped the pretense that the landing pad was relevant, it still proved to be a convenient meeting place.

The Redheaded Devil's last known location was as good a place to start as any. Beav and Estep were confident that they'd find clues to lead them back to an earlier time in that man's life. And from there, they'd go back earlier. And so on. Even better, if they could get their hands on his brain, they could access the Redheaded Devil's database and find his origins that way.

That's why they hoped that they'd find the Devil unconscious like he'd been when Estep (and afterward Serena) landed on him. Their plan was to work fast and sedate him before he regained consciousness. They'd bring him back to GSI, retrieve his teleportation database, analyze it, and voila! There was an excellent chance that they would finish this mission swiftly and easily, without ever seeing the whites of the Devil's eyes.

None of them thought that Serena Wilcox needed to be a part of this. This wasn't an investigative or fact-finding mission so much as retrieval. If things went haywire it would become a military operation, which was all the more reason to leave Serena out of it. They left for the Redheaded Devil's domain without considering the idea that they should check first to see what Serena and Mandolin were doing.

Natalie Buske Thomas

28

Serena waited for him in the dimly lit kitchen. Her children and husband were sleeping right down the hall. She felt the hairs on the back of her neck stand up. She knew he was there before she turned around.

"S-s-s-serena," he hissed.

Serena spun and then executed the front round kick she'd spent hours perfecting. Caught off guard, the Devil backed squarely into Mandolin. Mandolin grasped him in a choke hold that rendered him unconscious. "Way to go, chica! I told you we could take him down. One, two, me and you. That's all we needed."

Tom and the kids hadn't even woken up. The incident was over in a flash and relatively quiet. Serena hugged herself. "The sooner he's out of my house the better."

Mandolin agreed. "I'll shoot him up with this." He pressed a syringe against the Redheaded Devil's neck. "There now, done. He's all ready for transport. I'll let them know I'm dropping him off."

He phoned Beav and got no answer. He tried Agent Estep next and had the same result. He tried Eduardo, even though he couldn't say he cared for the man. Eduardo answered on the first ring. Mandolin explained the situation and got approval to bring the Devil in. He wasn't going to kill him. He'd let GSI decide what to do with him. Once he delivered him, he considered his job done. He left the Devil with Eduardo and intended to go home.

He had a nagging feeling that something wasn't quite right. He did a U turn, screeching tires and all. He headed back to Serena Wilcox's house. He saw two silhouettes in the window. At first he thought it was Serena and her husband in a private embrace. He blushed and started to back out of the driveway. Then he saw the smaller figure drop to the floor. He jumped out of the car without even putting it into park. He ran toward the house, but he was too late.

When he opened the door, Serena Wilcox was gone. Tom had woken up and he had reached the living room in time to see his wife disappear. The Devil stood alone in their living room.

"Where is she?" Tom grabbed the Devil by the lapels.

Mandolin struck the Devil on the head, sending him down as fast as his clone had fallen. He didn't have another syringe, but he didn't need it. He'd whacked him hard enough that he'd be out for a good while. He lifted the unconscious man and leaned him against the foyer door. He turned to Tom. "I'll get her back."

Tom said, "That's what you all say. *I'm* getting her back, and this time I won't let her go."

A sound from the kitchen made both men jump. Serena peeked into the living room archway. "Aww, I love that you want to rescue me, my husband."

"You're OK?" Tom looked her over. She seemed perfectly fine as far as he could tell. There wasn't a scratch on her.

"I'm giving up on the 'damsel in distress' thing. The first time around I beat the Devil. When he came back with his clone I teleported out. I got a bite to eat and came back."

Mandolin grinned. "Good for you, chica. Kick-ass heroine."

"Well, only because I knew you were taking care of it. I was kidding about getting a bite to eat. I was worried about Tom and the kids. But," Serena hugged Tom. "I can't quit GSI."

Tom said, "I'll support you either way. I just want you to be happy, and safe."

"I'm stronger than I think I am. The thing is, GSI is going about this the wrong way. They're chasing after the Redheaded Devil, again. They haven't even thought to inform the men from the 'future beyond'. They risk alienating our first ally in this new intergalactic world without time and space borders. Americans have a reputation for being cowboys and I'm afraid we're living up to it. It's the wrong move, absolutely. I need to reach our mysterious new friends before Estep stomps through the universe in his big muddy boots." She looked at her husband and added, "Come with me, Tom."

Mandolin said, "You won't even know I'm there unless you need me."

Tom said, "What will I have to do?"

Serena reached for his hands and led him in a waltz around the living room. "Dance with me upon a star."